Tholan

MYSTIC PROTECTORS SERIES BOOK 6

KATHI S. BARTON

This is a work of fiction. Names, characters, places, and incidents are products of the author's imagination or are used fictitiously and are not to be construed as real. Any resemblance to actual events, locations, organizations, or persons, living or dead, is entirely coincidental.

World Castle Publishing, LLC
Pensacola, Florida
Copyright © Kathi S. Barton 2018
Paperback ISBN: 9781949812220
eBook ISBN: 9781949812237
First Edition World Castle Publishing, LLC, October 29, 2018
http://www.worldcastlepublishing.com
Cover: Karen Fuller
Editor: Maxine Bringenberg

Prologue

Tholan watched his charge as she acted and danced on the stage. He knew better than to try and keep up with her — she was beautifully fast skimming over the stage. But she was stunning, and she knew the steps to the music like she did her own name. When the play she was acting in came to an end, he knew that she'd have to go to the back room and change quickly so that no one, not one of the other actors, knew that she was a female, not a male just as they were. Women did not act on the stage, nor did they sing and dance as if they were born to do so.

The men of this time thought it to be dangerous to have a woman act — which to Tholan was just silly. Some of them could and did play better and act better than their male counterparts. But Elizabeth was determined to be out there, showing her skills and having fun. And her father loved that she enjoyed acting as much as he did watching her perform.

When they had taken their final bow, he watched the others around her, making sure that none of them harmed her, and did not guess what secret she was hiding from them.

5

As they walked home, he encouraged her more, telling her that she was brilliant. Her face showed so much happiness for what she had done.

The streets were dirty. Even though there were piles of refuse and spoiled food along her way, she never turned up her nose at those that were digging through it. Some of the patrons of the stage had given her and the other actors hunks of bread and cheese. Even though her father and she could have used a bit of it too, she always shared her wealth with those that she knew needed it more than her. Her way of thinking was, she had someone to love her and a roof over her head.

Tholan wouldn't rest his protection of her until they were at her home. Her father was a good man, even though he would get into his cups a little too much. But he loved his daughter and the coin that she would bring to him nightly. They were a good pair, the two of them. While he'd never say a word to anyone, Tholan did think that he was in love with the beautiful Bethy, as her father called her.

Supper was the hard, crusty bread that she'd saved a hunk of from today, with tomatoes sliced thick and salted heavily. There was broth too, with just a little of the potato that they'd had last evening, and a bit of fish, left over from the supper the night before that. It smelled good, he supposed, but it wasn't something that he'd eat.

Poor didn't describe the way these two lived. They did have food once or maybe twice a day. There was always tea, though there were times when she'd use the leaves over too many times. And wine for her father. It helped, her father told her, with the pains in his legs.

Tholan knew from her father's protector that he wasn't long for this world. His legs, both of them in sad condition, were rotting off at the knee. And as there was no coin for the doctor, they lived their life as well as they could.

Taking her father out on the stoop, a chore for one as small as herself, Bethy sat with her father, telling him of all the things that had been in the play. They were the same stories, her changing them up a little for freshness, and she told him that no one, not a single person, knew who she was.

"I'd hate to think what they'd do to someone as delicate as my little flower." Her father touched his old and callused hand to her cheek. "I've heard tell that they stone a woman who would dare breach their rules. You be careful, my Bethy. I should just die without you by my side."

"I am as safe as you are locked away all day whilst I am gone. And if they find out, I think—nay, I know—that they'd do nothing more to me than to push me aside and have a man take over my role." She laughed—it sounded like tinkling bells to Tholan. "Though I doubt anyone could do a good job of it. They all sing like men, and the voice that I have is much lighter on the ears."

At bedtime she tucked her father into his cot. Then she did what she did every night to keep them safe—Bethy put a large stone in front of the door and stoked up the fires. Sleep would come easily for her, Tholan knew. It was exhausting to her to keep up with acting, as well as helping her father around.

The next morning, Tholan was there when she rose up. He whispered to her that it was going to be a grand day. That she would be happy though it was raining hard. Going with her to her father's bed, Tholan saw her shake him hard, and when he didn't move, Tholan looked at Michael, who appeared in the room with them.

"He has passed. I've come to take him home, as his

protector has been assigned to someone else." Michael came to get all those ready to pass. It was a difficult job—he was forever busy in his role—but Tholan was more concerned with his own charge. She was taking the death of her father very hard.

When the undertaker came to take her father's body away, Bethy cried harder as he was put in a wagon with the other dead. Tholan's heart hurt for her. He knew that her own had to be broken badly—her father was all that she'd had in the world.

It was a hard time for so many now, food being in such short supply. The diseases ran through the people quickly and without care to age, or how the ones left behind were to deal with it. There wasn't any money for a proper burial for most, and Bethy's father was no different. As she walked behind the wagon, she kept telling her father how much he had meant to her, how she was going to miss him so much.

Tholan was beside her with each step, telling her that she'd be all right, that time would heal this wound for her. He could not touch her, could not do what he wanted to do more than anything. And that was to take her into his arms, under his wings, and hold her until the world, her world, was a much better place.

That evening he tried to tell her not to go to the theater—a grand name for such a hovel—and that they would not miss her for one night. But he also feared that if she did not go, she would sit in the house and not eat or drink. The things that she did there, on the small stage, made her happy, and for that, he supposed, it would be a good thing for her to do.

Her face was swollen, and Tholan told her to say that she'd had a cold. No one would question her about her father—they all thought her to live alone. That like them, she had no one.

When she dressed herself in her garb, Tholan told her how lovely she looked, whispered that there were none prettier than her, and their voices were not nearly as nice.

The play went on. Mistakes were made—they happened every night. But when it was over, instead of going to the pub with them, to celebrate another night of merriment, Bethy gathered her things, all of them, and made her way home.

The roads were slightly cleaner than they had been on the way in. The rain, hard and driving at times, had washed the worst of the dirt and trash away. But it was slippery, the stones and mud making her step very cautiously as she walked along.

The wagon for the dead was making its way along the streets again. She moved to walk to the other side of the road to avoid it. But as she was making her way across the wet stones, she lost her footing and tumbled down. Tholan was reaching for her—to do what, he had no idea—when she sat up.

"I have fallen." The people roaming the streets just stared at her while she laughed, and when Bethy stood up, still holding onto the wagon that was near her, she started crying. "I wish it to be me in this cart this night."

Her hand came from the cart to her head. That was when Tholan noticed that her hand was covered in blood. Standing close to her, trying to see if she'd been hurt badly enough to need help, she looked at him. Tholan stood very still when he thought her eyes were staring directly at him.

"Hello." He nodded. "I've fallen down. I think that I've rattled my head. Do you suppose you could help me along? I don't wish to be alone tonight. I might join my father, and I do not wish to die alone."

Before he could tell her that he had her, someone moved

through him. A man, tall and big, grabbed her hand and tossed her to the road. The blood that poured from her head this time was pooling beneath it.

Scooping her up so that her soul could be taken now, Tholan made his way to the other realm. He didn't want her to hurt, but it was much too late for that. As soon as he summoned Michael, he knew that something more had happened.

"What have you done, Tholan?" He explained to Michael that he'd brought her himself. "But she wasn't to die. Not yet, at least. She has many years to go. Children to birth. Generations to bring to the world. You have taken her too soon."

Boss came to see him as he stood there, her lifeless soul in his arms. He took her from him, his anger so strong that Tholan flinched back from him. The woman had not died, that was all that his mind could center on.

"You have taken her too soon. Do you know the repercussions that you have caused this day? The things that have to be changed, children that will not be born? What will happen now, Tholan? What of the generations and generations of children that were to come from this woman and her husband?" He asked if she could be taken back. "Nay, it is much too late for that. The man that you took her from, she was meeting him today. He would care for her in her need, and they would love like none other. You have done her and the world a misdeed that will be felt forever. You must explain to her what you have done."

"I cannot." Boss woke the soul in his arms. The woman looked at them all but didn't say anything. "You must be able to take her back. You are all powerful."

"In this, I cannot. You have— Words fail me on this. You

must tell her what you have done to her." Tholan backed away. His own heart was broken too. "Michael, take care of him. I shall have to see what I can do to rectify this for her. But the timeline for her, it is forever broken."

When he disappeared with Bethy, Tholan lay on the ground, his wings spread out over him. It was his death that awaited him. Michael would surely kill him now. And when nothing happened, he looked up and saw that not only had Michael drawn his sword, but he looked ready to use it on him.

"You must die as well." Tholan nodded, his heart, his mind no longer able to function. "You have killed a human. One that was set to be the mother to a great many special people. Do you have any idea what must be done to fix this? If there is even a fix?"

"No, my lord, I do not. I thought her dead. There was so much blood under her. The man, he threw her to the road and he—"

"His fingers slipped. He was helping her to rise. Her mate—that was her mate for all time, and you have done them all a misjustice, Tholan. All generations, not just theirs, will feel this forever. You deserve to die."

"I do." He waited for the blow, the one that would remove his head. It was no less than he deserved.

Tholan thought of the woman. Bethy was no longer. He had no idea how Boss was going to make it so that she could go back, but it would never be the same for her, or for the man who had only wanted to help her.

Michael ordered him to stand and Tholan, confused, did so.

"You will go to your cell and stay there. No contact with anyone, not on Earth or in this realm, for a period of one

11

thousand years. And when you return, if I allow it, you will not be a protector as you have been until such time that our Lord feels you have paid the price for what you have done. Go. Get yourself out of my sight. You have nothing to say that I wish to hear."

Michael, his friend, turned his back on him. It hurt him more, Tholan thought, than if Michael had removed his head. Willing himself to his cell, he laid upon his cot. His life, his life as a protector, was finished.

~*~

Thousands of years later

PJ and her da loved watching old movies—the older the better. And when there was a marathon with their favorite actors, they would binge on them until they were cross-eyed exhausted. But they had each other, and they were happy. And PJ loved her da more than she did anyone in the world.

"Angela said that she was going to go and get her hair done. That was two days ago. I wonder what sort of fluff and cut they do on dogs such as herself." They both laughed. Da had married Angela six years ago, when PJ had been a teenager. Now they just tolerated her, both of them. "I will have to do something about her soon, I think. She has made things difficult for me at the board."

"Like what?" PJ knew that she was to take over the company when her da retired—if he ever retired. "I was in there yesterday and got caught up on the paperwork, by the way. And you should know that I've also invested in the school that we talked about."

He nodded. Da, Parker Daniel Brooks, was a hell of a businessman. And in turn, she had learned from the best. The business that he'd purchased for a song before she'd been born had turned into a multibillion-dollar industry, leaving

12

them both room to make more investments and even more money for them—not that they needed it. But they were very generous with it, and that was why they continued to make more.

"I guess she told Milton, and you know how he can be, that when I passed away, she'd be taking over and he'd be gone. He told me that he didn't think she'd do a good job, not as good as you would." PJ was already shaking her head. "You have to take it, PJ. You want her to spend all our hard-earned money on getting her nails done and other men?"

"No, but I also have enough on my plate for now. And besides, Da, you're going to be around for a very long time." They both laughed. When the doorbell rang, neither of them moved. "You and I, we have plenty of time for us to make any kind of decisions on what is going to happen. You won't leave me anytime soon, will you?"

"I hope not."

PJ stood up when someone cleared their throat. It was the police, and they looked like they meant business. "Can we help you, officers?"

"Mr. Brooks, we're here to arrest you for armed robbery and murder." PJ looked at her father, a man confined to a wheelchair since she'd been born. "You have the right to remain—"

"Hang on there, young man. I don't know what's happening here, but as you can tell, I've no way of robbing anyone, much less holding a gun. I don't own one, and wouldn't know how to use it if I did."

But they took him in, with her following the cruiser closely. Angela had come in just as they were leaving, and was pissed as well.

Booking him for a crime that he'd not done, nor could

possibly have committed, took nearly three hours. By then they'd shuffled her da from one end of the station to the next. Each place they'd gone, someone had asked him about the chair, and every time they told them that he'd been in it for years.

The next morning, they told her that he was going to go to trial. It seemed to her that things were being rushed through, and Da's attorney was trying his best to get them to understand that her da didn't do this. All the while, PJ stayed by his side until they took him to his cell.

"They're ramming this through, PJ, and I haven't any idea what I'm supposed to do. And if they're doing this to him now, I can't imagine what they're going to do to him during the trial. I cannot get anyone to tell me where this thing occurred or how it happened. I'm worried for his safety." Joseph March, her father's attorney, looked as if he'd aged several years over the last twenty-four hours. "It's as if they're trying to blame this on him for some reason that I can't fathom."

"Will he go to prison?" Joseph told her that it was looking more and more like that all the time. "You mean before the trial. They'll get him to prison and what? Forget about him? This is all Angela, isn't it? She's doing this so that she'll somehow end up with Da's money."

"I didn't want to say that before, honey. But to me this has the markings of someone desperate." He looked around and then leaned into her. "I don't know what is going on with her, but your father told me that he thinks she's put out a hit on him. If this is her way of getting him alone, then she couldn't have worked it out better for herself. And if he's convicted, she can perhaps get out of the pre-nup that she had to sign. She'll be able to say that he lied to her or some such nonsense, and that will be the end of Brooks."

Her father had worked hard on making his way in the world. She knew as well as anyone how much he'd given up, how much he'd scrimped and saved to make this work for the family. And now this. Looking around the jail, she asked Joseph how many years he thought her father would get — if he were to make it to the trial.

"The max he could get for murder and armed robbery is twenty years, I think. I don't know how they think to make this stick, but then, this entire thing has me baffled. The least amount? I don't know. Four to ten?" She nodded and thought of what she had done already and what she'd have to give up. "What are you thinking? You thinking that he'll make it?"

"I did it." Joseph asked her what she'd done. "This thing. The thing that they have on Da. If I confess, then he can't be charged. If I confess, then he's free to find out what happened and see if Angela is a part of it."

"No. You can't do that, PJ. If your father got wind of what you're thinking, he'd bust your bottom. No. That's a terrible idea. Don't even think that again."

PJ nodded and told Joseph to listen to her. "I'm younger than him and able to get away should someone come after me in this place. And Da has a good attorney in you. The two of you can work together and set things right." Joseph told her again that this was a bad idea. "Then if you have a better one, I'm all for it. This will have to work, Mr. March. If not, then I'm going to lose more than just my da's business; more importantly, I'll lose him. And I just can't do that."

"Let me talk to him first. See what he thinks." PJ told him no, that if he did, he'd talk him out of it. "PJ, this is not a good idea. You're only twenty-three years old. You have a good head on your shoulders and have become a good attorney in this short amount of time. If you go to prison, you'll lose that as well."

"I'm going to save my dad. The details in this, they won't matter because Da doesn't have what it takes to live the life of a prisoner. I'll just confess and let the chips fall where they might. You and my dad, you can get me out. If not, then he'll be all right and I'll come home to him when it's all said and done. That's what has to be done, Mr. March. We both know that there isn't any way that he can survive this. He's too frail. And being in a wheelchair, they'll hurt him with that as well. Please. You have to help me with this."

It took less time than she had thought it would for her to be jailed. Her father was released and barred from seeing her until the trial. Everyone, including her stepmother, was pissed that she'd confessed. And confessing in front of a news camera had spoiled a great many plans, she thought.

The trial was just as she'd been told it would be—quick, no evidence. The witnesses that the police presented kept saying that they had seen a large man running away from the scene after the place was robbed. No one had a name for the man that she'd allegedly killed, and there wasn't a body. Things like this, whatever they were doing, were going to be something for the books one day.

Four days after she confessed, not only had she been found guilty of the crimes, but she'd been shipped to prison. Her da cried during the entire trial. PJ knew as soon as the trial began that there wasn't going to be any saving her. She was going to go away for a long time.

Ten years. Ten years for a murder there wasn't a body for. Ten years for a robbery that she didn't do, as well as ten years of life without her da. PJ had been fucked. And there wasn't anyone who could help her.

Chapter 1

Parker read over the last of the reports that had been given to her. The businesses were doing well. She was just putting away some of the files that she'd pulled out when Allen Blackwell, her personal attorney, came into her office. He'd been in and out of it since she'd arrived this morning.

"I've made a dent in the things that you handed over last night. I have two bids on the downtown apartment building that I think you'll be pleased with." She asked him about the other. "That is going to go just as you planned. How on earth did you know that she'd not paid her taxes in all this time?"

"Because she's used to having someone do shit for her all the time. Plus, she's broke. And when I was going through some of the records that Da kept, I found that she'd been paying them with his credit cards, and that had stopped. Once he passed away, the courts canceled them all and she was shit out of luck." Parker grinned at Allen. "You didn't tell her, did you?"

"No. But she'll be served in a few hours. Also, those buildings that you wished to purchase downtown, they're

17

sold. I'm sorry. And I've a meeting with the owner tomorrow. I made it then so that, if you should want to go, you'd have time to clear your morning." Parker, no longer PJ since she'd gotten out of prison two months ago, told him that she would love to go. "Good. From all accounts, he's a good man. Rich too, so perhaps he'll allow you to buy them from him, as he and his wife and a few others that he works with own most of the rest of downtown. Especially after you tell him what you want to do with them."

"Mostly I want it to turn them into something better than it meant to me. That is the building that the robbery and murder that I 'committed' happened in. I need to get in there, before someone tears it down, and see what I can find. Did you know that there hasn't been anything remotely business-like in there in the last twenty or so years?" Allen knew that. Parker was also looking over some records that she'd found in her father's desk. "I have some things that I'd like for you to take care of before tomorrow. And I need to make a few donations to the charities that have sprung up in town. Do you know anything about the charity work called Business Helpings?"

"Just that it's a project of a couple of people, one of them being the wife of Riss Trainor. She's been coming up with a few nice projects like this one." Parker asked what they did. "It's a great set up. They have other businesses come in and interview people who might have been out of work for a while. Or some kids that need a first-time job. They also set them up with nice used clothing, as well as a ride should they need one. After that, they will help the people get to and from work for six months if necessary."

Parker liked that. Some of the women that she'd been incarcerated with had never had a job, their skills at computers

18

were usually nonexistent, and they didn't have anything but the shirts on their backs. Prison, for some, was the only way to have a roof over their heads, food in their bellies, and for the most part, hide out from someone trying to kill them. Parker had seen it all.

"Good. That's something I can get behind. And I'm to understand from Maggie that there is a clothing drive as well as a school drive. See what you can find out about how I can donate to those causes as well." She marked the things off her list that she'd wanted to go over with her attorney, and then leaned back in her seat. "I need to revamp the kitchen here. Can you find someone to help out with that?"

"I know just the firm. It's called Heavenly Starts. I have no idea why, but it's a bunch of men and women, most of them just needing something to do with their time, that can get a job done in no time. And I do think that they're a part of the other firms here. They don't charge you but do ask for a donation to one of the charities that I mentioned. And before you ask, yes, it's all legit. Good things are coming from your new neighbors, Parker. I'm glad to be helping them out with you."

She made herself a note to check them out as well. Not that she didn't trust Allen; he'd been helping her for the last eight years on keeping things running here. But she did want to check it out. She might find something that he'd not noticed.

"The new computers you asked to have donated to the schools have been delivered. Just as you asked, no one knows who they are from. And the Internet has been set up for the place in the same way. The old computers, they've been donated to the local shelters, just as you asked them to do." She nodded and made another mark on her list. "I'd like to take you to dinner tonight. There is a restaurant that I think you'd really enjoy. And it's a part of the family that is doing a lot of updates in town."

"The PP&J place." Allen grinned and nodded. "Maggie has talked about nothing but the bread that she gets from there every day. And two days ago, she brought me a roast beef sub from there. Holy shit, it was great. Okay, I'm in for dinner. I have about three hours of work left here, then we'll go."

"No, we go now." She looked at Allen and cocked her head. "You'll be here till midnight again, and we both know it. About ten, Maggie will come in with something for you to eat, which you'll ignore, then you'll get up at six in the morning and forget to eat because she's not here to remind you. We'll go there now, Parker. If we do, you'll be able to last longer on a full stomach."

Laughing, she got up and followed him out of the house. Stopping to tell Maggie where she was going, she was given an order for three loaves of bread, bagels, and if they had some, muffins. Parker asked if she was able to eat too.

"Go on with you. Seeing you going out, even if it is with this old man, is better than you sitting behind your daddy's desk all night. He'd be mightily upset with you if he could see you now." Maggie hugged her tightly and told her to have fun. "And don't forget my order. I'd hate to not have anything here for you to eat in the morning."

The place was packed when they got there. Parker still hadn't gotten her driver's license renewed and hated to have to rely on others to get her around. There was the limo, of course, but that was just not something she was comfortable with yet. Being in the house alone for the most part was difficult enough.

"Mr. Blackwell, it's nice to see you again." The young

man seated them and introduced himself to her. "My name is Kip. I'm going to be your server tonight. I'm kinda new at this part, but my mom is working here so I thought I'd help out. What can I get you to drink?"

He was personable. His charm, if that's what they called it now, was right there and it made her smile. It was the first time since she'd been out that she'd had a meal in a restaurant, and because of him, she wasn't as put off as she thought she'd be. Ordering an iced tea, she sat back to have a look around the place.

The walls were done well. She had a feeling that someone had either a good hand in art or these were the original wall advertisements. There was a counter at the front that had pastries and breads in it. And toward the back, there was rack after rack of jams and jellies. Parker could smell the fresh bread baking, and it made her mouth water. When a glass with ice was set before her, she was astonished that a pitcher of the most beautiful amber colored tea was set down as well.

Judith, the owner, came to sit with them, and was talking to Allen like she'd known him for years and years. When Parker's sandwich came, she could only stare at it. The size of it was about three times as much as she'd expected. Not to mention, it was about five times bigger than what she could eat.

"Something wrong with your sandwich?" Parker told her that it was a tad bigger than she'd thought. "Yes, well, we have a lot of elderly come in, and they love being able to share then take some home to share for the second time. And we're happy to have their business. You're Parker Brooks."

"Yes." She pushed the sandwich away and Judith pushed it back, telling her to eat it. "I'm not much on being out in the public yet. When people recognize me, I sort of seize up, if you can imagine."

"You are the woman that supposedly killed a man and robbed his place. When Allen mentioned you, I had my friend, Dusty, look into a few things. She has this freaky ability to find and track people. I've been finding a few things out that perhaps your attorney should have found." Parker said that it was a slam dunk when she'd confessed. "Yes, so I heard. And your stepmother, Angela? She needs to have her ass kicked about a dozen times. Right to the edge of town, and then pushed out."

Parker laughed. It was nice having someone that was so honest with what they wanted to say and just said it. She picked up her sandwich that had been cut into fourths and bit down into the crusty bread and rare roast beef. After telling her that it was good, Parker asked her about her interest in her trial.

"Oh, for any number of reasons, I guess. But mostly because no one seems to know who you killed. And the place you killed this unknown person in has been empty for a few decades." Parker said that they had wanted her father. "Yes, well, I'm to understand that instead of leaving his riches to his wife, he left everything to you. Smart man, your father. But I'm betting that there was more to it than him just being a smart person."

"I think so as well." Judith got up to leave them but said that she'd return. Parker looked at Allen when he laughed. "I'm assuming that you knew this meeting was going to happen, and that you somehow set it up that I'm going to be meeting more of the group that I want to do business with."

"Yes, well, I've had some trouble getting you out of the house. And this way, not only do you get to see the people that you want to do business with, but you also got some food in that skinny body of yours." She looked down at her waist and then back at him. "You have lost a great deal of weight, Parker. And none of it was by design. I've also been informed that if you sit here quietly, you'll get a show while you eat."

She had no idea what he was talking about until Angela walked in the door. She'd not aged all that well, and Parker had to cover her mouth just to keep from laughing out loud. The fashion plate that she'd always been was gone, and in her place was a haggard looking woman who looked as if she'd been binging for several months, and not on salads.

"I wish to speak to the manager." Judith was in the back room, more than likely by design. "She said that this bread was gluten free, and I just read that flour is a gluten. I want my money back."

"That is our *rice* bread and made with rice flour, which is gluten free. Besides, I don't think we can give you a refund on that." Angela, her voice very loud now, asked her why not. And in an equally loud voice, the cashier answered her. "You've eaten all but an inch of the bread, and that isn't enough to return. I can get you a refund on this much." The cashier laid a quarter on the counter and walked away.

"Why, of all the nerve. Get back here." Parker stood up, and Allen asked her if she was ready for this. Angela continued to berate the poor girl as she made her way to the cash register. Angela was on a roll now, it appeared, and was screaming at the top of her lungs. "You tell that woman that she's lied to me for the last time. I want her to come out here and face me."

"Angela?" Angela turned so quickly that she nearly fell off her too high heels. Parker looked her up and down and smiled. "I see that you've let yourself go. I'm guessing that all the sex you had in my father's house kept you in better

23

shape than one would have thought. And so that you know, most flour has gluten in it, but not rice flour, as she told you. Moron."

When Angela drew back her hand to no doubt hit her, Allen grabbed it in midair and told Angela to behave. Her screaming had the entire place standing up and staring at her, just the sort of attention that she loved. With Angela going on and on about bread and Parker being an ex-con, just out of prison, Parker listened to her before Judith came from the back room.

~*~

Tholan heard about the uproar at the deli. He wished in a small way that he'd been there to see it. He'd run into Angela during his time around the town that the compound was in. She wasn't the type of person that he thought of as a nice being.

His charge was a nice young man. He worked hard, and his business was doing well. Jack had a pleasant family, two of the cutest little girls, and he didn't seem to be into anything that would get him into trouble. The only time that Tholan had to give him encouragement was when his mother-in-law would come to visit. The poor gentleman would be so depressed after she left that he'd sit in a dark room and cry.

She would say things like "Can't you get a better paying job so that my daughter doesn't have to work so hard?' Jack worked two jobs so that his wife didn't have to have a job outside of the house. And she seemed to have everything that she needed, even if he had to work just a little more to afford it for her. "I wish that she'd never married a lazy ass like you." Tholan was trying to wrap his head around that one. Jack seemed to be at work more than he was at home.

And the one that would send Jack to the basement for

a few minutes to compose himself was, "Your mother must have slept with her brother or father to produce you. You are far and away the stupidest man I've ever had the misfortune to meet."

He never commented back to her, but his wife did. She would order her mother out of the house, which wasn't enough as far as Tholan was concerned. The woman, to him, should have been barred from the house forever. But he wasn't in charge.

They were in the basement tonight, the mother-in-law having just been ordered from the house, when he moved closer to his charge. Tholan wasn't sure what to tell him that he'd not already said to him but wanted him to get some encouragement from the fact that she'd been told never to come back. Tholan had a feeling that even the children were relieved. She had been taking her nastiness out on them when she could no longer get to Jack.

She was getting to him — that was the problem. He'd had to tell him nightly before this that his life was worth living, and that taking someone so precious from his family would be a heartbreaking thing to do. But now, Tholan couldn't hear his thoughts. Nor could he see any sort of expression on his face. When Michael showed up, Tholan wanted to beg him to not kill him, to let him do this, when he shook his head.

"I have sent his children down to him." The two little girls came down the stairs then and crawled up into his lap. It was the first expression that Tholan had seen on Jack's face for many hours. "His wife could use some of their kind of loving too, but him more so."

The smile was there, but it was a sad one. At this point, Tholan would take what he could get from him. Moving closer to the chair where they sat, he told the man again how much

25

the little ones would miss him should he do what he was thinking about. Just as he was ready to walk away, Tholan tried something else.

"You will take your family on a long vacation. You must use your vacation hours at work soon or you will lose them. One hundred-twenty hours; that is a great amount of time for you to be resting with the children and your wife." Jack paused in hugging one of the daughters. "You have been saving for something special. This would be the perfect time to tell your wife that you have been offered that promotion and the house in another country."

"Would you guys like to have some fun?" But girls screamed in delight, and a genuine smile came to his entire face. "Yes, I'm going to talk to Mommy, and we'll get things all set up tomorrow. What do you say?"

They were still screaming and laughing as he took them both up the stairs, one on either arm. And when he found his wife crying in the kitchen, he told her what he'd just thought of. Tholan was so excited that they'd be getting away that he almost forgot that he'd be going with them, in a way.

By the time they were going to bed, Jack and his wife had narrowed it down to three places to visit, in addition to the place he was being sent after they returned. His wife had told him, numerous times, that she wasn't telling her mother. She was finished with her.

Tholan wasn't sure that was a good idea either, but for now, he thought, it was what the older woman deserved. When his nighttime replacement showed up, Tholan was glad for the rest. It had been a stressful day, but he thought that it turned out well in the end. As he sat in his room, he thought of all the changes that had occurred since he'd been released from his cell so long ago.

When someone had passed, Michael would have been the one to bring them over. It had been easier for him, as the watcher would simply go to someone else that was born. But as the world got more and more crowded, it became too difficult for Michael to even get away, much less help with the new guests. Instead, it had fallen to the ones that had stayed with them their entire life.

In the long run, Tholan supposed that was better for both. The watchers would get a short reprieve, something much shorter than it was now, and no one was lost in the waiting for Michael to be free. There were other things that had changed while he'd been confined to his cell, but Tholan knew about them. There were meetings that he was to attend, but not interact with the others. That was harder than he'd thought it would be, as he'd had little to nothing to do with the others anyway.

Not to say that he didn't have friends; he did, but not that many. Riss had been someone that he could go to after he'd been released. Tholan was thankful every day that he'd not been beheaded. One thousand years of being in his cell was much better than being no more.

Tholan decided to head to the compound where the others were. As soon as he was there, he knew that something had happened. It seemed that everyone was on edge, and he wasn't sure that he could help—or for that matter, if he should even get involved. Boss stepped in front of him almost as soon as he decided that he'd find Riss.

"I have a favor to ask. You may say no, Tholan, but I have this woman that needs to be watched for a little while. Her watcher, he is exhausted from watching her. She rarely sleeps, and when she does, it's not for very long. If you would just go and sit with her for a bit, I'm sure that her watcher would be very appreciative." He told him that he'd be pleased. "Good. As I said, she rarely sleeps. Her sleep pattern is still on prison time, and I think that she is working hard on something for her father, who passed while she was behind bars. But she needs someone to keep an eye on her."

"I would be honored." Boss took him to the office where the woman sat behind a desk that would have been suited for someone much larger. She had to stand to reach things on either end. "She is very unhealthy looking, if you do not mind me saying so."

"It is her lack of sleep. As well as the fact that she has a great deal on her mind. If you would take a look at the notes that she has to do, you'll see that she has a great deal on her plate. Or so she thinks. I think it will take her a little while longer just to realize that she has many that would gladly help her." Boss looked at him. "She's much like you, I'm thinking."

"I have asked for help." He felt his temper, not in a good place of late, seem to rise up a couple of notches. "I have been nervous, as you know, of being a watcher again. It has me feeling as if I might fail yet another person."

"You won't, Tholan. This I can promise you." He looked at the woman with Boss. "She took the fall for her father so that he might be able to find out why he was accused of something that he could not have done. Neither did she commit the crime, but before he could find out what was going on, he passed away. She misses him like she would an appendage or her heart. And then there is her stepmother. A vile woman."

"She thinks her involved? In the fall, as you called it." Boss explained to him what he meant. "Oh yes. I can see where— This is the woman, I'm betting, that caused the trouble at the deli where Judith works."

"Yes, that's the one. She has caused a great deal of trouble over the last few days. And it will get no better before it ends.

That is why I worry so about this one. She has been through more than most, and I'm afraid that it will break more than her heart before all is done." Tholan could see the sadness there when she looked up from her work. She had lines beneath her eyes, and her lips were puffy from biting them as she was doing now. "I'm thinking that she needs a friend."

"She has none?" Boss said that she'd only been released from prison a few months ago, and that the ones that she had before left her alone. "I would be her friend. I know what it is like to be confined. I deserved mine, and so much more. But she, she is innocent of what she was accused of."

"What an excellent idea. You could be her friend. Would you do that for me?" Tholan wasn't sure what he meant but nodded anyway. He'd do anything for this man, even going to the point of laying his life on the line for him should he ever need it. "I will fix it so you have a place. Wait, you've purchased a home. You could go there."

Before Boss left him at his newly purchased home, Tholan had an idea that he had agreed to something huge. But Boss, he was as happy as he'd ever seen him, and there wasn't any way that he was going to take back what he'd said he'd do. Now all he had to do was figure out what it was. Lying in his own bed that night, the one that he'd purchased online, as Jenny had taught him to do, he tried to think where he'd volunteered for something. But Tholan was too excited to think for very long. Whatever he was doing, he'd give it his best.

Chapter 2

The meeting was running late. Not that Parker minded all that much—all she'd do when she got home was sit in her office and work on paperwork. This was only the second time in three months that she'd been out of the house. Yes, both had been about her businesses, but this time, there was a friendliness to it that made her catch herself smiling once in a while.

She thought of the meeting at the deli yesterday. Angela had been a horrid person to the young woman, but the cashier gave as good as she got. Parker thought that if she'd done that, had the balls to stand up to her stepmother before going to prison, then things might have turned out differently. But yesterday had been a real eye opener on all kinds of things.

Judith hadn't taken her shit either. That was what had Parker smiling off and on for the last several hours. When Judith came from the back room, her apron tied about her tiny waist, Parker took a step back, knowing that Angela was going to go down, and she was glad to be there to witness it.

"Listen up, you moronic fuck. You ever talk to one of my

31

employees again as you just did, and I will rip your throat out and then piss on your dead body. And if you think, in that tiny fucking brain of yours, that I'm joking, then try me." Angela told her that she'd lied to her. "I most certainly did not. First of all, I can't lie to anyone; secondly, you're a fucking moron, as I'm sure I've said to you numerous times before. If you'd done your research, as you claimed that you'd done the last time you were here, you'd know that rice flour does have gluten in it, but very little. And again, the research says that there is no such thing as gluten free bread. Flour must be added to make it work. You got your refund, now—"

"Well, I'm not satisfied with my so-called refund either. That person only gave me a quarter. I paid six dollars for that bread, and I want a full refund." The cash register was opened and Angela smiled, like she'd won. "There. See, I told you that the customer was always correct."

Judith laid a second quarter next to the first one. "That is all you're going to get from me. If you have a problem with it, which I'm to understand from every establishment along this block is normal for you, then call the cops. I'd very much like to tell them about the can of green beans that you returned for a refund with one bean in it because it wasn't the same size as the others. Or the bottle of lotion that was returned nearly empty because the straw was too short for you to get the last few drops out. Bring it on, bitch. I've had enough of your bullshit, and so has everyone that works here."

Parker had laughed, which brought Angela's attention around to her again. "You bitch. What business is this of yours? Why are you even out, anyway? There is no way that you could have gotten out for good behavior. I know what you are and what you've done. Besides, I thought murder was a life sentence. The nerve of some people trying to act as if they belong in normal sociality. And then you tried to blame your poor father."

Her voice had been loud — the entire room had turned to look at them. Parker felt like a two-year-old again, her hand caught in the cookie jar at home. But this was so much worse. This was not just embarrassing, but it hurt her in ways that she'd not felt before.

Parker glanced at Judith and the woman winked at her, and suddenly some strength that Parker needed surged upward. Looking at her stepmother, Parker felt as if she could take on the world.

"You never loved him or me, did you? You only wanted what he could offer you. A home, money, security, and money. You will notice that I have repeated the money part, won't you, Angela?" Parker laughed. "But he got you in the end, didn't he, stepmother dear? He took every bit of it away from you and gave it to his ex-con of a daughter. And you want to know what else? Da did it long before you set him up to take the fall for something that never happened. He knew what you were the day after you wed him, and he caught you fucking the delivery guy in his bed the day after the honeymoon."

"He did not catch us. And we didn't do it in his bed." Everyone in the room made a sound, reminding Angela and her that she not only had an audience, but she'd also just confessed to sleeping around. "You're going to pay for this, PJ. See if you don't. You'll see that I'm going to get what I deserve, and you're going to hand it over to me with a smile."

"Oh, I have no doubt that you'll get what you deserve. You see, I've been doing some research on the happenings that put me behind bars. And once I can connect the dots — to you, I'm betting — you're going to be spending a great deal more time behind those same bars, but for a lot longer than I did."

The punch to her face knocked her on the floor. Parker started to get up when Judith held her in place. She told Parker that if she played her cards right, Angela would be behind those bars in about ten minutes. All she had to do was press charges.

Angela was taken away, screaming that Parker had hit her first, despite witnesses to the contrary. And while the blood on her lip and nose wasn't that bad, it was there, while Angela didn't have a mark. As soon as she was out of the place, the entire room erupted in applause. Everyone, it seemed, had had enough of Angela Brooks.

"I'll meet with you in the morning with the rest of the gang." Parker had a cup of tea, which tasted of heaven to her, while Judith explained what she wanted to do. "I think we can work together on a lot of projects coming soon. And if you'd like, and even if you don't, I want to help you find out what had happened to have you ending up in prison. I have some abilities that will be able to help you out."

"I'm working on it now. Things are beginning to add up, but I don't have a starting point nor, other than me being in prison, an ending one." She told her about the building and all the other shit that she'd been finding out. "Angela set us up, I know that. Figuring out how is the hard part. But I'll get there."

"I'm sure you will." Judith packed up some things in a large bag. "Your cook, Maggie, called here. She asked that you bring home a few things. Also, I put a tin of that tea you're drinking in there. You and I — I think we're going to be good friends."

And now, here she was in the deli again before it opened,

having a meeting with five of the most beautiful couples that she'd ever seen. Parker was a little overwhelmed by them. They were happy, in love, and they touched a great deal, something that Parker had missed while away—the hugs and the love of her father. If not for the prison computers, she wouldn't have had any contact with anyone much.

"The building that you're wishing to purchase isn't for sale. But, anytime you wish to go inside it and look around, take tests or whatever you wish, just go ahead. None of us are using it at the moment. But I do have plans to turn it into an apartment building for dislocated families. Mostly abused adults and families." Agon, the owner of the building, winked at her, and Parker could have sworn she saw a twinkle in his eye. "But, I was going to suggest that you not own it anyway. People, the wrong sort of people, will think you've only purchased it so that you could go in and make it look like you wanted it to look. Like you were innocent. And while I know that you are, the cards, as they say, must be played out legally."

"I had actually thought of that. But it's great to hear it confirmed. Neither my father nor I committed those crimes, and I'd very much like to pin it back on the person who set us up." Valyn said that he'd want to do that as well. "I'm not positive that Angela did it, but I'm finding things that are pointing the finger at her."

"She did it." Parker looked at Judith. "I told you yesterday that I had some abilities. We all do. What I can tell you will only help you, not get her taken to prison. And I looked and can tell you just what she did and how she paid for it. Well, paid for most of it anyway. Blackmail."

"The police commissioner." Judith nodded. "Okay, that explains the arrest. But the rest—the judge that sentenced me;

the speed in which it happened. That, I'm assuming, is the same thing, blackmail, but I can't find any connection to them all."

"As I said before, you'll get it. But I have a question. You didn't even bat an eye when I told you that I have abilities. Nor when I mentioned that we all have them. So, I'm guessing that you have some contact with people like us at some point in your life." Parker just nodded, not sure where Judith was going with this. "But, I'd say that you don't know what we are. Or, if you do, then you're not sure about it."

"I have no idea what you are, no. None of you. As for contact, a couple of people that were inmates with me, they were a tiger and a bear. But they wanted to be behind bars. Said that they thought themselves safer there. Their mates had been killed, and rather than join them, they put themselves into a situation that put them behind bars. And no, I didn't ask." Riss said that it happened all the time; they get tired of life alone and wished to just live out their days in solitude. "Yes. That's what they said. That ending their own life was harder than they'd thought it would be, and they wanted someone to care for them that had no vested interest in their lives. Sort of sad, but I don't judge people who like it quiet. I do as well."

"This is a family that doesn't do quiet well, as you've noticed." Parker told Riss that she had noticed that. "We're Mystic Protectors. And in order to explain what that is, you have to know that we were once protectors—beings that watched over all the creatures of the earth until their deaths. Most of us had been to the point of wanting to end our existence. But we were asked by Boss to come here and train other protectors so that they could do their jobs better."

Parker wasn't sure if she believed him or not. But when

the men stood up and spread out wings behind them, Parker stood as well. She wasn't sure what she was going to do when she was asked to have a seat again, but she was positive that she had hit her head somewhere along the line.

"No, you didn't hit your head. We can all, should we want, read your mind. Everyone's. Usually we don't—we don't want to intrude—but I was worried that you'd freak out and I didn't want you to run." That had been her intention, so she didn't even try to deny it. "Are you all right with the rest of it?"

"No. Not just yet. Just let me have a minute." She *was* freaking out. And she wanted to tell them that she'd seen someone before with wings, but his had been black. Arryn, in a very excited but fearful voice, asked her when she'd seen him. Getting up, she started pacing the room. It was that or run. "When I was arrested. It was—let me think. I was in the jail, yes, but they had put me in a room where I was all alone. Or so I thought. Then this person—something—came into the room. No. That's not right either. He was there, in the two-way mirror, but not exactly in the room with me."

When no one spoke, she turned and looked at them. They, in turn, were looking at one another. Parker was no longer freaked out—now she was terrified, because they looked terrified.

"Do you remember what he looked like? His face?" Parker nodded slowly but said nothing to Valyn. "It would go a long way in helping us figure out who he might have been, or if we've taken care of him yet."

"Taken care of him? Why do I get the feeling that this thing, this person thing, is something that you've dealt with before? Or at least something like him. And not only that, but you have reason to believe that this wasn't just a 'one of' thing." This time they all shook their heads. "I see. Actually, no I don't, but I think I should go home."

They all screamed "no" at the same time, and Parker sat down. She wasn't told to sit, but if she hadn't, she would have fallen on her ass. Sitting there, she tried to remember every detail about the thing that had been there.

"He had dark wings. I'd not call them black, but they were close to that. They were also drippy, like they were still wet, their color not yet dried enough to let the true color come through. I remember thinking at the time that they were bloody, but I dismissed that. I don't know why, but I think it was just easier to think of it like that rather than any other way." Riss asked her to go on. "I don't think that it was just male, now that I reflect on it. Sort of both. His eyes were black. Not just the irises, but the entire orbs. There were no hands to speak of, just long stick like things that came from his shoulders and chest, like a spider. He had eight of these things like a spider would, but he wasn't standing on all of them, just the two."

Closing her eyes, she looked in her memories for what the thing had looked like. It was something that she'd done in college when a test would be coming up. It had helped her a great deal, and gave her the ability to graduate with honors, three full years before she should have been able to.

"I can look, if that will help. You'll never know I was there." She asked Riss for one moment. Please. "You're doing a very good job, Parker. Thanks so much for this."

"His face. He looked like someone that I know — or knew. The appendences, they were sharp like I said, but they also had this green something on the tips. At the time, I thought that it was poison. I still do. As I looked around the room for the thing that was reflected there, I realized that he didn't want me to see him. The trick of the mirrors, I guess, was what let me look. I was staring at him and he knew it somehow. It startled him, more than seeing him did me. After a few seconds of us staring at each other, he moved. But the door opening had him looking to it. The scream. It screamed loudly when he looked at the person that came in."

"It was because of me." The others took a step back. Not in fear like she had thought, but to give themselves room. The spreading of their wings again, all of them, had her standing up and reaching for something to protect them with. A sword filling her hand made her feel better, but the man, he gave her comfort somehow. "Hello, Parker. Your father says to tell you that you're doing a good job in getting information on Angela."

The world didn't tilt, as she'd read happened to people at times. Nor did she feel as if she'd been swallowed up. Parker just blinked out.

~*~

Kala was pissed, more than she'd been in some time. As she wiped the blood off of Parker's head, she glared at Boss. Of all the stupid things to do, he'd frightened the poor girl. As if she'd not had enough happen to her over the last decade.

"I didn't mean to scare her, Kala. I felt the moment that she was going to remember me. I thought it only fitting that I show her that I was on her side."

"By scaring the bejebbes out of her? Or were you trying to make a point? I'd like to know what that was if you don't mind." He just shook his head, and she had a feeling that he was trying to hide his laughter. "I do not think this is the least bit funny. What if she had hit her head and died? Then where would we all be? Tell me that."

"She's mated to Tholan." That shut her mouth. "Yes, I

can see that I've slightly redeemed myself in your eyes. And though they've not met yet, not in the flesh, I've taken the liberty of making her as immortal as the rest of you."

"Parker isn't like him." Kala wondered what he'd been thinking to mate a woman like this nice woman to Tholan. "She'll eat him alive."

"I don't think so. He's sort of met her. I have asked him to befriend her, as a human friend. He's still trying to figure out what he is going to be doing for me, but he brought it up, her having no friends, and I thought he'd make her an excellent one. And before you ask, he has not thought of her as anything but a woman that has been hurt." Kala asked him about the need for sex. And how powerful it was when mates came together. "I have delayed those feelings as well. I think that they will make good friends, do you not?"

"I don't know." She looked at the bump on Parker's head and glared at Boss once again. "You could have told us. Don't say it. I know what you're about to say—what fun would there be in that? But Tholan is afraid of his own shadow since he's been working again. I think this might be a mistake. I know you are all knowing, Boss, but with this, I can't see it working."

"It will. Simply because they need each other. More so than even the combination of all your needs, all the rest of you put together, and how much you need each other, even now, Kala."

Parker moaned, then sat up. She looked at Boss, then at Kala.

"You're all right now." Parker told her that she wasn't sure. Then she looked at Boss. "This is Boss. He's the man that we all work for."

Parker looked Boss over, like she was studying him for

flaws or something. Kala wondered what she'd find, because there wasn't any doubt that she'd find something. And when she stood up, they both did as well.

"You might be boss, but you are nothing even close to being just the man they work for, are you?" Boss shook his head. "That thing, the creature that was there that day, you not only know who he is, but what he is as well, I'm thinking."

"Yes, he's an underlord. I've yet to figure out what he was there for, you or someone else, but there isn't much that I can find out about the other realm without causing a stir. And since I have no name, other than what he looked like through your memories, then I cannot go there with my suspicions." Kala asked Boss if he had an idea. "Sadly, I do not. Parker saw him longer than I did, and he was nothing more than a poof of evil when I entered the room."

Parker moved into the dining area from the back room where they had brought her. The shop was open now, and they were serving a huge crowd when she made her way to the juice counter. Asking for a large smoothie, Parker stood there looking out over the crowd as Kala and Boss approached her.

"He looked like my father, but he wasn't. And I know for a fact that it wasn't him. My father wasn't an evil man." Boss said that he wasn't, no. "I also think I might know his name. He said it once. But I could be wrong about that as well. But before I tell you that, I'd like something from you. A favor, so to speak."

"I can grant you just about anything, my child. Just tell me what it is you want."

Kala wondered about the favor too. She had never bargained with Boss, and she didn't think that anyone else had either. She would simply ask, and he'd either tell her that it was coming, in the works, or in due time. Any and all of which meant that she wasn't getting it just yet. But with Parker, he'd willingly told her that she could have it.

"Did you really talk to my father? Never mind. You would have. Is he all right? I mean...I don't know what I mean, but is he all right?" Boss laughed and said that he was telling anyone and everyone that would listen about his baby girl, and how she'd stepped in where no one else would have. "Yes, well, I did figure that I could survive prison better than him. And it only seemed like they were looking for a body. I, however, think that taking me somehow messed things up for the person in charge."

"And you would be correct." Parker took her tall smoothie to a table — after trying to pay for the drink and being denied — and sat down. As she sipped it, she mumbled to herself. Boss looked at her. "She's always done this. Talked to herself to try and figure out a clue or an answer. She's very good at it, but people think her nuts. Or that's what she thinks."

"My favor — may I ask you for it now?" Boss nodded at her with a smile. "I'm sure you already know, but I'd like for you to keep everyone that I've been working with safe from this creature and Angela."

"I can keep most everyone safe from her. But I would think that you'd not care so much if Angela was safe from the people that she's working with. People, I'm sorry to say, that are close to you." Parker looked at her and Kala shook her head. "Nay, she does not think you are going to plot against her, my dear Kala, but she worries about you and the other women. I think she should have a demonstration as to how protective you are. Oh, and your sword, should you need it — you should also be aware that it is there for you to use. Just raise your hand, think of it, and it will fill your hand. Your knowledge on how to use it, you have that already, don't you?"

"An elective in college. So there is someone working with Angela that works for me." Boss didn't even so much as blink at her query. "I might even know who that is. Thank you. The creatures name, it's—"

"Don't say his name. Not here." Kala looked around and noticed that no one was looking at them. "I will come to you in your slumber. You will tell me then."

"Yes, all right. But I have to warn you, I don't sleep well, nor all that much. And when I do, there are all sorts of nightmares that I'm sorting through." Boss told her that she needed a friend to unload on. "I do. But not these people. I like them. And what I dream of, it's not PG rated. More like triple x. Too much sex and horror to even want me to speak of it."

"I understand." Kala did as well. She also knew what sort of dreams Parker would be having. Not the precise ones, she'd bet, but close.

Kala had had her share of them lately, and she wondered now if the rest of the women were. At Boss's nod, she knew they were. It was time to gather the wagons, as someone she knew used to say. And what better way to gather them than to have a meeting? One that introduced Parker to Tholan. A way for their friendship to start to bloom.

Don't push. Kala huffed at Boss when he left them there. Parker was getting herself some lunch and another smoothie when he spoke to her again. *This is a good idea, my dear, but don't push them together. They will both push away faster should you do that.*

Are they really suited? He said that they were perfectly mismatched and would have a strong happy life. *That does not instill any kind of confidence in me. Not where Tholan is concerned.*

43

I want him to be happy. Both of them to be. But I have my doubts that together they can accomplish that.

Trust me, Kala. You'll see that I'm right. She'd started to tell him that he was always right when the other women entered the deli. *You will have a nice afternoon, get to know each other, and bring up the dinner. Everyone will be like you, disbelieving that they're suited. So, I do not have to worry about them letting the tiger out of the bag.*

It's cat. But then, when I think on it, it just might be tiger. I have a gut feeling that both of them have been holding back for some time. And when their powers are released, even their love, it will blow the rest of us out of the water. He told her time would tell. *I'm buying you a frigging watch. That way you can tell me a time rather than that stupid thing you say all the time.*

He was still laughing when he gently closed the connection. Kala wanted this to work, if for no other reason that she wanted everyone to be as happy as she and Riss were. When they all gathered around the large table, the argument between Parker and Judith about paying for her meal made her think that Boss might really be right. There was a tiger in Parker.

Chapter 3

The dream started out horrific. As she was trying her best to run from the spider that she'd seen before, something or someone was always there to tell her where to hide, where to turn. She had a feeling that she knew who the help was, and when Boss appeared at the end of a long hall, Parker ran to him with open arms.

"His name, Parker." She whispered it in his ear as he held her to him. She might have been a little leery of the man—there were all sorts of things in her dreams that used the faces of those around her, but none of the protectors. So of course, she found it hard not to trust who Boss was. "Remember what I told you. You have something that will help you harm him enough to slow him down."

Then he was gone, and turning slowly, she saw that the creature was there, not a foot from her. He smiled at her, as if he'd won. Thinking of the man whose face he had taken, Parker felt her back stiffen, her heart calm as she reached for the sword as she'd unknowingly done before.

"You think to slay me, little girl? You are nothing against

45

my power. Do you have any idea how much I will toy with you? How I will play with you before I take you as my own?" She didn't speak to it, knowing that somehow it would give him power over her. "I have all the power I need over you, Parker Jane Brooks. And I will have what was promised to me. Soon."

All she could think about was that someone had promised her to him, and that he knew her name. So when he lashed out at her, his spindly leg nearly touching her face, she swung the sword as she'd been taught with all the power she had.

The scream hurt her ears, but Parker was afraid to put her hands over her ears for fear that he'd attack again. The small sliver of his leg smoked and burned on the floor. When he reached for it, she jabbed at him again, not hitting him but having him leap back from her.

"You think to keep me from my parts? You are nothing. Give it to me and let us go to my home." Parker laughed. It was the first time in a very long time that she felt it race over her body. Confidence like she'd never felt before had her stabbing toward him again. "The next time we meet, we will be on my turf, you insolent child. When I have you in my clutches, you will rue the day that you ever touched me."

"Bring it on." She started to call him by name, but a thundering no, which sounded just like her father, had her snapping her mouth closed. "Go back to whatever rock you slid out from under, you piece of horse shit."

He moved toward her again, and she touched her foot on the piece of him. This scream was not as painful, and Parker had a feeling that Boss had done that for her. When the creature was gone, she looked at the small piece of the thing that was still there.

Taking off her socks, she put them both on her hand and

picked it up. It smelled terrible, and there was something about it that made her want to destroy it. Or better yet, just leave it where it was. But she also thought that it would come in handy at some point and felt herself being dragged awake. Opening her eyes, she looked at her hand and saw that the nasty thing that she'd had in her dreams was just a stick now.

"Now what to do with it." She had to hide it, knowing that the thing would want it back. She was not sure why, but Parker had a feeling that it was going to be a useful tool at some point. Looking around her father's big room for a place, Parker remembered the safe that had been installed in the floor.

It had been put in right after her da had had this room redone. He'd been wanting to do it for a while, so when he'd had the carpet replaced with hardwood flooring, the safe had been the perfect thing to put in. Getting up, holding the stick still with her socks, she pulled up the big area rug covering the safe.

The combination was her birthday, and as soon as she opened it, she knew that Angela hadn't found it. Or if she had, she couldn't get it open. Putting the socks and stick aside, she pulled out the things that her father had put inside.

It must have been difficult for him to do this. His wheelchair would have had to been moved out of the way and him lying on the floor to open it. She wept as the things were pulled out. Some of them were things that she herself had put in, thinking of the things as treasures at the time.

There was her dolly, the one that her father had gotten her when she'd turned five. It looked like her, from her red hair to the freckles across her nose. Putting it aside, she pulled out the box, a metal one that she knew her father had opened just before he'd passed away. The sticky note on it was dated two days before he'd passed.

There was a copy of the will that had been sent to her in prison. A transcript of the trial, as well as a list of names. Reading over it, she saw that it was a list of witnesses, as well as the people who had been at the trial each day. Laying them both aside, she sat back and opened the box. The letter atop of everything inside was addressed to her, and also dated two days before his death.

My darling daughter. I miss you more and more daily. I'm not going to make it so that I might hug you in my arms once again. I'm sorrier about that than I am anything that I've ever done in my life. You were and will always be the owner of my heart, and I wish, just once more, I could tell you face to face what you've meant to me all these years.

Leaning back on the footboard, she wiped at the tears that started to flow the moment that she'd seen his handwriting. Her da had a floral type writing, like what you'd find in older letters. He told her once that if you were going to take the time to write a letter, you should write it in your own hand and put as much effort in the style as you would what you had to say.

I'm dying, as you well know. And I'm not long for this world. But I will be watching over you, so behave yourself, my child.

Laughing, she read on.

And don't be brooding in the house all the time. Get out, be young, and have fun for me. I will come back and haunt you if you don't.

Parker thought of the people that she'd met. The way that they'd taken care that she didn't sit around the house all the time. It was actually making her feel better, and her mind clearer about the things she was doing for the town. Looking at the letter, she wondered if he was really watching over her and flipped to the next page.

Angela did this to us. And when you confessed, something that I wish you'd not done — but was necessary, as I've come to realize — you made her mad enough that she destroyed several dresses of hers, keyed one of the cars, and screamed for an hour. It was the best time that I've had at someone else's expense in a long time. But back to the things that she's done.

There are a few people that you should no longer trust. While I could have fired them, I thought at the time it would be easier to keep them closer rather than out where they could do us more harm. One of them is Joseph March. He is in on things with Angela deeper than I first thought.

Parker got up and left the safe open. She needed to make notes, and there was nothing in this room to do so. Her da hadn't a television in this room, nor a desk. To him, a bedroom was for sleeping — nothing else. So she'd left it his way. Taking a shower, she thought about March. Parker knew that he'd been killed about a year after her father had passed away. She made a mental note to find out how he had been killed.

If he had been in on it, which she had no doubt that he would have been, that explained where Angela had gotten money enough to buy her house. Parker would go over bank records more closely now and see just how much they'd been able to skim. It couldn't have been too much at a time, or she would have noticed it right away when she'd been studying

49

them.

Getting dressed, she picked up everything that had been in the safe, put the stick in it—again with her socks—and closed it. Then she opened it again, returning everything that had been in it. No one would guess that it was there, and she wanted to keep it that way. Parker made her way to her office first, then to the kitchen. Maggie was there, as she always was, making the kitchen and sometimes the rest of the household smell wonderful.

"I've made you a light lunch, child. Lady Kala called here earlier and said that you were to come to her home early—by four, she told me." They both glanced at the clock. It was nearly noon now. "I'm glad that you're getting more sleep. You should try and sleep in more often."

She hoped never to sleep like she had last night but didn't stay anything. Parker didn't really want to have dinner with them. Not that she didn't care for them, but as it had been pointed out before to her, they were loud, huggy, and they didn't take no as an answer very well. All in all, she just wanted to be left alone. But that wasn't helping her with her life right now.

"I have some things that I'd like to box up and get out of the house. Not a great deal, but some of the furniture that was left in the house when Angela was moved out. Do you know if there is a charity place that might take the clothing?" Maggie told her that she'd look into it. "I don't care if they tear the clothing down for the material. Angela never had good taste in clothing as far as I was concerned."

"She never had good taste in anything if you ask me. Did I tell you that before your wonderful father passed, she wanted me to put him on a low carb diet? The doctor himself said that your daddy needed carbs more than anything, him being so skinny at the end. Stupid woman. Did she think I'd not ask him before I did whatever she wanted? I'm glad to be rid of her." Parker said that she was as well. Maggie huffed, something that she'd done since Parker had been a child. "Oh, I'm to tell you that the tea that you got from the deli? It's going to be brought here, as well as other breads and pastries. I've had a bit of it, and it's very good, isn't it?"

"You drink as much of it as you want. And yes, it's delicious. I guess Judith makes it, along with jellies and jams. She explained to me what the difference is, and I enjoyed an hour just taste testing what she makes. I might put on some weight if I go there too often."

Maggie told her that she could use it, and Parker just nodded. Her weight was the least of her problems right now. Someone had promised her to the *bug*—what she'd decided to call it from now on—and she needed to find out who. But first, she wanted to finish the letter from her da.

After telling Maggie about the workers and giving her the phone number that she could call, they decided what they wanted in the room and what other room could use some updating. For sure the dining room. The floors needed to be redone as well as the walls painted.

Parker loved the living room, but Maggie had been right in pointing out that she needed to bring it and the television that was in there up to this century. It was one of those tube televisions that, if she remembered correctly, still only displayed black and white pictures. She and her da were not big on sitting around watching television. They made use of the projector and screening room when they watched their favorite old movies. She'd not watched one since she'd been gone, she only just realized.

It took them the better part of two hours to get that

finished up. Then she had to get ready to go to the Trainor home. Tomorrow she was going to take her driver's test over and buy a car. It was time to sell the ones in the garage; her da's babies, as he'd called his cars, were too painful to have around. And she thought someone else might enjoy then more than she would.

As one of the limos was brought for her to ride in, she thought of the stick again and why Bug hadn't made a bigger deal about her having it. She supposed that, like her, he wouldn't want her to think he needed it. But for some reason, Parker knew that he did. Now she had to figure out who she was to tell that she had it. And that would be no easier than anything else she had on her plate at the moment.

~*~

Warrior hurt like he'd never hurt before. And living here, in the hells of—well, Hell—he knew real pain when it hit him. But when he looked down to where his finger should have been, all he wanted to do was go to the child and kill her. But he would have his. Warrior knew that as well as he did his own pain.

Hiding his hand in his robes, he made his way to the common area. He had had permission to go above grounds. It had been his duty to go and retrieve two people that had been sent to them. But he just could not give up the chance to see what the morsel he'd been promised looked like. Entering where she had been—the prison, they called it—had been forbidden to them all.

Parker looked like a dream. And her body made his cock harden, his mouth water, and his need to fuck her off the charts to have her under him. Or above him. He cared not how he had her so long as he could. And he would too. Very soon.

Six years ago, he'd been assigned to pick up a woman who had died in an accident. The woman was wonderfully messy. Her head had been split open, both of her legs mangled to nearly coming off. Even her torso, the meat of her belly, had been spilled out onto the seat she was on, as well as the floor of the car.

Touching her enough to wake her brought her up and at him in seconds. The fight of her had him leaning her over and fucking her into what he had hoped was submission. Warrior didn't care if his partner enjoyed a good fucking or not, so when she screamed out her release, he nearly came a second time, just feeling her squeeze her pussy around him. Then he turned her over.

The part that he had taken looked nothing like the mess in the car. But he'd not realized that this body, his part, was old, and used up. Ugly, he thought she might be called. And she berated him for five minutes before she struck a bargain with him. One that he wished now he'd acted on when he started this.

To have waited for six years for his prize, while the body got to walk around, was hard on him. There were rules about going into a prison and taking someone. But he did go to the mother's house, fuck her with his real body, and leave her in agony several times a week until he grew tired of her grievances. She did that well too—complained all the time.

"You let me live forever and I will give you my daughter. She is beautiful. Like me." He nearly removed her head—he didn't think her pretty at all except for her body. "She has flaming red hair. Mismatched eyes, one blue the other green. And a body to die for."

"But you said that she looked like you. And I know well enough that you have not had a red head that did not come from a bottle. Your body is old and saggy, and your eyes are the same color as shit, the revolting stuff that humans void out when they've eaten too much." Warrior didn't know if that was why they defecated; he just knew that it was a vile habit that he didn't want to ever pick up. "Is this paragon of beauty yours or not?"

"She is. I swear it." She asked if she could retrieve her phone. When she pulled it to her and flipped around in it, he had a moment where he thought that this would matter little. If her body was found before they struck a deal, then all would be lost. Then she turned the small instrument to his face. "Look at that face. Is that not the face of a beautiful woman that can satisfy your every whim?"

The woman in the picture did look like she could take a hard pounding. And she would give as good as she got if she was anything like her mother. Warrior asked for her name, thinking to trick the human into being taken and him having the girl too.

"No, no names until we make a deal. I want to live forever. Be healthy and never catch any diseases. I don't want to put on weight, nor do I want to hurt. All that for the girl." He thought it over, the way that she worded her demands. It was just too easy, but he put out his hand and agreed.

Warrior was sure that she thought not to shake on it, the deal that they'd made. But he took her hand in his and marked her. Marked her with his mark that also told of their bargain. That the child of this woman was his, and none other. When she screamed in pain, he put her back in the car and gave her life back. The only way that she could be killed now was by him, or someone stronger than him. He liked it that way too.

Now he had not just his prize's name, but also her birthdate. This was going to be a real coup for him. As soon as he had her, he was going to present her before the king himself. Rollin the Warrior was going to be thought well of forever after this.

He had thought of taking her himself. Thought hard on it at the time he was promised her. But he also knew that his predecessors had done that, thought to hide the females from their lord. Warrior wasn't stupid enough to think that he was better than them, nor smarter on how to get her by him. He knew that he couldn't. So giving her to him as a gift would pave the way for everything that he'd ever wanted.

"You smell of the otherworld." Warrior looked at his cellmate and sneered at him. "You have been told to bring back bodies for us, not to galivant around like you own the place."

"And how is it you know what I've been doing? Tell me that, Peck." His name was Peter, but Warrior enjoyed calling him Peck. "I know my job and I do it very well. Have you heard of me getting into trouble? You have not. And would you like to know why? Because I do not cause it. Now, be gone with yourself. I have things to attend to this day."

His hand was hurting him badly now. Warrior moved to his room and laid on his cot. He hadn't any idea how to mend himself. No one had ever fought him back before. And whatever that creature had used on him, it wasn't normal. Pulling his injuries from his robes, he looked at his stub.

His fingers were gone, with most of the top of his palm. It had sealed when she'd hit him, as if it had been colder than anything that he'd ever encountered before. But it was more than that. It was as if she had had help, from the king of her realm.

"No. No, there is no way that she had that kind of help. I have her, and I have her fair and square." He'd been wanting to use that phrase since he'd heard it on Earth the other day. Now that he had, Warrior had no idea why he'd thought it was so wonderful. "The things that humans say when they are telling me why I shouldn't have them. It borders on insanity."

Now he had to figure out how to explain what had happened to his hand. Because even though he was going to be on the up and up about the woman, losing a piece of himself was against their laws. And to have left it behind as he had, it was going to get him into serious trouble.

"I'll just go back to her dream state and get it. There isn't any way that she has the power to pick it up. And if she were to do that, then she'd really be marked as my own." Then there was the added trouble that if she had picked it up, someone on her end might be able to tell her what it was. There were protectors and watchers all over the place where she resided now. "There is no point in borrowing trouble where none has presented itself."

Another human saying, but this one made sense to him. There were all sorts of them that he'd heard over the decades of being the delivery person. Some made no sense at all, like his least favorite—pretty as a speckled pup under a little red wagon. What the fuck did that mean?

Did the person just call you a dog? And why was a mongrel pretty? They smelled, licked their own asses, chased their own tails, and drank from the portal that humans took a shit in. Then there was the wagon. A thing to carry about goods wasn't pretty. It was useful. He had—

His door opening had him leaping from his bed. Too late he remembered to hide his hand. When it was jerked toward Merlin—such a stupid name if someone were to ask him—he whimpered slightly before dropping to his knees and begging for forgiveness.

"What have you done?" He told him that he'd been collecting and went to check on his prize. "You don't even have the sense to lie to me, do you? Do you have any idea what caused this? What sort of magic was used to make this mark on you?"

"I do not wish to lie to you, my lord. I have seen what it did to others of my ilk that have done so. I was made a bargain, a good and solid one. And when I went to check on her, only in her dream state, she attacked me." Merlin squeezed his hand again, which had him screaming in pain. "My lord, I have no idea where she got it in her head to harm me. But I made a good bargain and was going to bring the morsel to our king as soon as I collected her."

"Why have you waited? If she is, as you say, for our king, then why have you not brought her to us?" He told him of her being in the cell, the one that he wasn't to enter, and that she had only just come to be released. "A prison, huh? Then she is to come here anyway. Why was a bargain struck, and by whom?"

"Her mother. She said that she killed the prize's father by setting him up. And that she, the mother, wished to be rid of her for only a longer life. She had other requests as well, such as she should not gain any weight. But I have taken it upon myself to make her saggy, but no weight gain. Then there is the—"

"Enough." Merlin looked at his hand and gave it another squeeze before letting it go. Warrior didn't make a sound out loud, but he was screaming in his mind. "You will not go— Where is the rest of yourself?"

"I left it behind." Whatever he had expected, laughter wasn't it. Merlin, not known for a sense of humor, laughed for a good minute before he shifted, his body no longer that of the form that everyone was used to. No, he had become himself, his royalty as well as his beast. "You will return to get it now. And if it is gone from the place where you lost it, you will stay above ground and find it. Of all the— Do you have any idea what would happen to you should it fall into the wrong hands? The trouble that this would cause, with the king of the Otherworld? He will not be happy. Nor will your own king once he finds out—"

"Please, I beg of you. Do not tell him. I will find it, this I will promise. I will find it and come to you first thing when I have it." Merlin didn't look as if he was going to allow him to leave after all. "I will find it, my lord. This I swear to you."

"You will, or the price will be more than you can endure." He knew that. Even Markum was still paying for his misdeeds. "Be gone with you."

Warrior found himself in the human world in the next breath.

When he'd seen Markum the other day, Warrior was sickened by his wounds, the way that green and yellow pus seemed to bleed from every part of his body. And where his cock had once been, burnt off by all the sex play that was heaped upon him, someone had put another cock in its place. But this one was made of a hot rod, one that would service anyone who used it, but would burn deeply into Markum's body.

"I will not have that happen to me." Then he remembered something from one of the rules that he'd been made to learn when he'd been created for his job. "I cannot be changed or have my head removed without being whole. If I do not find the piece, which I will, then I cannot be harmed as they have done to the others."

Chapter 4

Tholan was somewhat nervous. *Okay,* he told himself, *don't lie. You're terrified,* he laughed to himself. As he walked around the house of Riss, he admired the things that Riss had gotten to make his home homier, warmer, and more comfortable. One of the things that Tholan had fallen in love with was the fireplace.

There was no flame in it now, but he could imagine the warmth one would feel when it was going. And there were throw blankets on the backs of couches that seemed to warm the room up. Not by heat, just lying there, but with the warmth of happiness and comfort. He was admiring one such cover when someone behind him cleared their throat.

"You like the colors? I have earth tones all over my living room. My bedroom as well." He didn't know the young woman, not really, but he was looking forward to becoming her friend, as he'd been asked. "I didn't know anyone was in here. I was just taking a break. They're a lot, when they get together, aren't they?"

"Oh, my yes. I usually end up going back to my cell when

they become too much." She frowned at him, and Tholan tried to think what he'd said. "I'm Tholan. I have no last name. I was made to believe that you are aware of what we are. I'm very sorry if I offended you."

"You didn't, I guess. I was wondering if you were making fun of me when you mentioned the cell. But I'm betting that you really live in a cell, correct?" He smiled at her, feeling as if she might be able to understand him. "I'm Parker Brooks. I'm going to be a part of some of the projects they have going on around town. They're certainly making some good improvements, don't you think?"

She sat in one of the wingback chairs that faced the cold hearth. He sat in the other, trying his best not to fidget. He did that when he was nervous, and Tholan wanted to make a good impression.

"I've not spent a great deal of time in this realm. I have only just started watching someone again. I had been doing desk duty for decades." She told him that she had just hired someone to do that for her. "You are wealthy then?"

Her laugh embarrassed him slightly, but her face was beautiful when she did it. There was a sparkle to her eyes, and the lines around her mouth were no longer there in those few seconds. Tholan thought that he could light his new home with the brilliance of her at this moment.

"Yes, I'm wealthy. My da and I, we worked very hard to make it so that we'd never have to be without when we needed something. Not that we suffered all that much before, but it is nice to be able to help out others." She leaned back on the seat, resting her head on the wing of the chair. "You do know that it's considered rude to ask about one's money, don't you?"

"I do now. That is one of those things that I have to work

on. When I need an answer for something, I've always just found it was easier to ask someone." She blinked several times, and he watched as she yawned. "I'm to become your friend. Do you think that would be possible? I don't even know how that works, friendship with a human."

"I don't have any friends. Well, the people here. And while I like them a great deal, they're overwhelming all together. I think I might have said that." She yawned again. "I've not been sleeping well. Since...well, since I was arrested. You know about that, don't you?"

The way that she peeked at him with one eye made him smile bigger at her. She was nearly asleep but working on talking to him as well. It was nice of her. And Tholan liked her all the more. As he watched her, she yawned again, and he could tell the moment that she drifted off. She was beautiful to look at awake, but simply gorgeous sleeping.

Her face was relaxed, her lashes fanned out over her pinked cheeks. Tholan saw her freckles then. They were darkest over her nose and upper cheeks, but he could spot them all over her face and throat. When she frowned, her mouth turning down, he wasn't sure what to think and crawled quietly on the floor to her. If she needed him, for whatever reason, he wanted to be close enough to do battle for her.

Parker squirmed a bit, her moans softly spilling over her moist lips. Reaching for her hand, wondering if he might be considered rude again, he touched his fingers to hers and saw what she was looking at. Tholan started to pull away when he realized that she was talking to a demon. A delivery demon, as a matter of fact.

"Where is my part? You will bring it to me this moment." Tholan wanted to step in front of her but wasn't sure what was going on. The need to protect her was stronger than he'd ever had as a protector for another human. The being began screaming at Parker, and Tholan realized that he should be paying more attention. "You are mine and will do as you are told. Or I shall slay you now and be done with your isomers."

"I think you mean insolence, dumbass. But it matters little to me what you're trying to say when I know that you cannot take me until I am dead." The demon said that he could arrange that. "No, you can't to that either."

She was guessing. Tholan didn't know why, but he knew that she was only guessing why the demon couldn't take her. Leaning close to her, he whispered what to say to him. It appeared to him just then that the demon could not see him.

"When promised to a demon, by whatever means, he has to have just cause to kill you. Like you've struck a bargain with another being, even his kind." Parker looked at him when the demon asked her what she was doing. That confirmed that he couldn't see him, and he felt braver for it. "Tell him that you will not be bullied. He cannot do that when you've been promised."

After she repeated what Tholan had said to her, the demon screamed and turned into his other skin. The large spider was bigger than a house, wider too. Not even counting his legs, he was that huge. That was when Tholan noticed that his front leg was injured and smoking. Parker had injured him. And not only that, from what he'd heard when he first arrived, she had that part of him too.

The demon left her in a puff of dark smoke. The smell of sulfur was strong in the air, and Tholan pulled from her to wake her. But as soon as he was in the living room once again, she looked at him. Fear, pure and strong, was written all over her face.

"I have you."

He was both shocked and happy that, when he pulled her from her chair, she went to him willingly. Her sobs, however, pulled at his heart in a way that he felt he would need to rub it to make it better. But as she continued to cry, he held her, telling her over and over that he had her.

When the others came into the room, hearing her crying, Tholan waved them off, telling them that he had it under complete control. Tholan had never had anything under control, much less completely so.

"Do you have wings, Tholan? The reason I ask, I wanted to know if yours were dark or white." He told her that his were white. "Good. I have no idea why it matters, really, but I had hopes that was how you told the good guys from the bad. You know, sort of like the hats that cowboys wore in the Old West."

"I'm not sure what that means. I'm not good at jokes either." He was trying to make her laugh, but she looked up at him, her cheeks stained with the tears that she'd shed. "I will not allow him to harm you, Parker. I will protect you."

"I haven't any idea why I know that, but thank you." He nodded, and she laid her head back on his chest. Not sure how comfortable she was, Tholan laid back on the floor, taking her with him. "As you've heard, someone promised me to that thing. I don't know who else knows, that but I'm sure that it was Angela."

"You would be correct." Boss speaking had Tholan wanting to sit up. But there was no desire for him to push Parker off him. She was his to protect. "When you told me his name, I didn't know that he would come to speak to you, Parker. For that I am profoundly sorry. I would have stayed should I have thought he'd be that stupid. But, as you have guessed, she did promise you to him. But I don't think that it will work for them, either of them, when he finds out the truth."

"Why is that?" Boss looked at him, and Tholan felt his defenses come up. Boss told him that there was no harm done when he apologized to him. "She is my friend. I should wish for her to be safe from this. And my Lord, she has a piece of him."

"I do." Parker sat up and he felt as if he'd been set in a freezer. Her warmth was something that he thought that he could bask in forever. "I've put it in the safe at home. No one knows about it. My da and I put the safe in when we had the room remodeled. It's amazing what you can find on the Internet. Anyway, he left me a letter too. I've yet to finish reading it."

"I would like to see the piece. But keep it where it is for now." She nodded. "With his name and the piece of him, it's a slam dunk that he's not playing fairly. And I have to tell you, I'm impressed with you. And with Tholan at your side, I can hope that you'll be safe too."

"He's my friend." Tholan felt as if he'd been handed the keys to the golden gates, he was so happy at what Parker told Boss. "I've only just met him, but I feel as if I have known him all my life."

It hit him right between the eyes just what she'd said. All her life. Their friendship was fast and solid. Tholan looked at Boss, and his wink did nothing to make him feel any better.

You could do worse, you know? Tholan nodded at the voice in his head. Michael must have been in on this as well. *Nay, not from the start. But the more I learn about this young woman, the more that I think she is the bravest and the strongest of all the others. You will come to love her, Tholan, and be her helpmate, just as she will you.*

I do not feel like I feel when touching the others when touching her. Michael laughed and Tholan snapped at him. *This is not funny. I did not want...I'm not going to tell you that I did not want a mate, I just did not want to hurt one.*

She will be hurt, my friend, but not so badly with you there for her. And you will be, will you not? Tholan told Michael that he would. *Good. I thought you would say that. Boss has...well, he has delayed the sexual feelings for the two of you. I did not understand it at first, but with the demon playing with her, I think it is best that you two are on your feet at all times.*

I believe that is toes, but I will be on everything to keep her well and safe. She is talking to Boss now. I should pay more attention, I think. Thank you, Michael, for telling me. I do not wish for you to be in trouble for telling me, but I do appreciate it. Michael said that Boss knew. *Then I shall thank him as well. She will be all right, this I can promise you.*

Of course, she will. I'm quite proud of you for helping her earlier with the demon, Tholan. Your knowledge — I had forgotten how well-versed you are in all the laws, including those that are with the other world. Tholan told him that it was his job. *Yes, to learn the laws of our kind. No one asked you to learn so many. You are a good man. And I now think, which I hadn't before, that the two of you will suit quite well together.*

Humbled, he thanked him again. And when Parker moved to the couch, so did he. He didn't sit right next to her, but close enough that he could touch her should she need him. Tholan had a mate. He wasn't sure what to do about it, but he was going to be her friend first. That, he thought, she could use more than she could someone kissing at her all the time. But he would have liked to do that, just once, Tholan thought.

~*~

The house was quiet when she got back. Maggie had long

since gone to bed, and Parker was exhausted as well, but had a few things that she wanted to take care of. Laying all the paperwork that she'd gotten from the others on her desk, she sat back and looked around the large room. She missed her da more and more every day, it felt like.

The letter, as yet unfinished, was in the safe. She'd not felt good about just letting it lay about for anyone to touch. She wanted to be able to take it to her nose, smell her father's cologne, as well as read it where she'd not have to explain herself. Going to her room that had been his when he was alive, she opened the safe, pulled out all the paperwork again, and got onto the bed.

She had thought about changing, perhaps getting into the tub to read it, but she didn't want to bother with all that. Parker just wanted to read the letter and take some notes on the little note pad that she'd brought with her.

Parker was going to read it first, then make notes about it secondly. Just reading the words, feeling all the emotions that her father would have put on the sheets of his monogramed paper, would be enough for now. Finding where she had left off, she settled into the pillows behind her and opened the letter.

Joseph was not skimming the accounts, as I had first thought, but he was taking things, mostly from the house when he'd come by, that he would give to Angela to be fenced. I'm not sure that they were having an affair. The thought of either of them in bed with anyone else sickens me. But if they were, that would explain a few things. But, smart man as I am, I closed that barn door as soon as I figured it out. He was no longer allowed to come to our home. On the pretense that I needed to get out more, I would meet him at a diner or such. But onward with this tale, my dear.

Two more people that you should no longer trust are Maggie and her spouse. As much as it pains me to write this, they too are skimming the pots, so to speak. The billing from the grocery has doubled over the last few months, since you've been gone, and I would very much like to say that I've taken care of it. Alas, I just could not bring myself to fire someone that makes the best biscuits I've ever eaten. But, while the amounts weren't high, only about four grand a month, it is something to be watching.

Parker thought of the renovations she was having done and decided to talk to Dan, the man that would be in charge of it all and have him give her all the billing information. Also, she planned to take Maggie's charge privileges from her. Parker wasn't above firing her or having a face to face about this. But she had held down the house for her while she'd been gone. No excuse for theft, but she would get to the bottom of it first and foremost.

Angela has some dirt on the judges that were at your trial. And I have come to find out, just recently, that some of the jurors had also been paid off, with a great deal of money. The police department will also need to be taken care of, as I'm sure you've figured out by now.

I wish that I could have taken care of these things before the trial, or even after you were taken away. But I had to find people that I could trust, and there are few of those around anymore. More than likely less so since you've been released.

How I wish I could have been there for you when you came home to me. I would have had a small celebration with you. Taken you to the finest restaurants and laughed over all the stories that you would have told me.

You are my heart, my child. Everything that I did was for you and I. I missed you so much at times that I felt as if my heart were broken, blood no longer flowing to it. I hope that you can straighten this out for yourself and me. I know that you can, but please don't be hurt. I don't know what I would do if I were to look down at you from my perch in the sky and see you harmed in any way.

I have more to tell you, my dear. But mostly I want to tell you not to let this make you hard. I should like for you to get married sometime, have children to fill that house that was much too big for just me. You don't have to name one of your sons for me, but I must tell you, it would be a real hoot to know that you did. I love you with all that I am, all that I will ever be, and more so than I have loved anything or anyone on this earth.

A man by the name of Benny Anderson has been by to see me several times over the last months. I would like for you to contact him as soon as you read this. (He cheats at chess. I'm telling you that so you know that is why I never won a game with him.) But he is a good man. A man with a great heart and a lovely wife. They're not human — not that that sort of thing ever bothered us — but I'm telling you that so that you will not be surprised by his wings. His wife, Lily Anderson, she is something special as well. Her wings are as pure white as my love for you is.

With all my love, your favorite Da.

"You're my only Da, you old poop."

Parker sat on the bed for another hour before she got up to get ready for sleep. Closing her eyes now was somewhat scary for her, but she thought of Tholan and how he'd made her feel when he helped her. No one had been that generous to her in a long time. And him being a complete stranger to her made it all the more special.

I am here for you, Parker. She looked around the bathroom, terrified out of her mind that it was Bug again. *Nay, it is I, Tholan. You and I have touched, so I can hear when you think of me.*

Why? Tholan asked her what she meant. *Why do we have this connection? I mean, it's nice, don't get me wrong, but why do we even have it? From what I've known about — well, shifters and such, sex or at least bodily fluids must be exchanged. As far as I know, we've done nothing more than you holding me when I was upset.*

'Tis enough. If you would rather I didn't speak to you this way, I can understand that. This is all new to you. I could also feel your sorrow. Did you finish the letter from your father? She wanted to demand that he not look into her mind, but that would be stupid. He was a good man, one that she'd come to enjoy talking to. And he kept her solid when all around her was falling down. *Nothing is falling down that you won't allow to. You're a strong woman. Stronger than anyone that I've had the pleasure of talking to.*

Sure, I'm stronger than the other women that you know. You think that Judith would sit on her bed and cry about her dead father? Doubtful. She would shed tears, I'm sure of that, but not like I have been. Like it's my job. He laughed a little, and she had to smile. *Now I'm being unreasonable. Are you sure that you still want to be my friend? I'm a little off my noodle right now.*

Yes. No hesitation on his part, and that too made her feel good. *As I have said, you're very strong, and it is my honor to be friends with you. You make me feel good about myself as well.*

In answer to your question, yes, I finished the letter from him. He gave me some names of people that I shouldn't trust. And two that I should. I'm also supposed to find a man by the name of Benny Anderson. I don't suppose you know him, do you? He told her that he did. *You guys, you like, hang out together or something?*

Yes. There is a compound on the property that Riss owns. It's huge, but magically so. There is a pool, some classrooms, as well as an exercise area. Not that we will gain any weight, none of us, but we do need to blow off water on occasion. She corrected him. *Then yes, steam. Though in my defense, I think they are the same. But the compound there is for several reasons. There are classes, as I said, and they teach protectors how to be more observant. To learn how to see things on a computer that we might not recognize or know what it is we're looking at. I'm thinking that you'd be good at that as well, helping out the other protectors.*

Doubtful. I'm barely holding onto my own life right now. Tholan told her she was doing fine. *I guess. I'm not going back to prison, yet anyway, and I've not gone screaming in the night when you guys pull your magical stuff on me.*

He was very quiet then, and she knew it was more than him thinking of something to say. It was more like he was thinking of a way to tell her something that was bad. Before she could ask him what he was going to say, he asked her if she was in bed or in her office.

I'm in my bedroom, but not in bed. Why? Tholan told her that he wished to come and see her. *I'd rather you just tell me what it is. I'm thinking that it's bad news.*

Nay, not bad. When she came out of the bathroom, he was standing in the middle of her bedroom. "Nay, 'tis not bad news, but something that I believe should be told to you face to face."

"Am I going to be pissed off?" He only shrugged at her. "I see. So, you think I will be, but you're hoping that I won't. Does this have anything to do with us?"

"Yes. You are my mate. And because of that, there have been changes made to your body as well as mine." He asked her if she could have a seat. "I should like to be able to leave quickly should you wish to take this out on me."

"Did you have anything to do with these changes? Or that we're mates?" Tholan said that he'd not. "Then you have nothing to worry about. Just tell me. And so you know, you're also going to tell me who made these changes to me without telling me about them."

"I will." He pointed to the bed and she sat down. "I am, as I have explained, a protector. The others, they were mated to their mates, the females of the family, in secret. Boss and Michael threw them together and let the feathers fall where they might. But in the end, as he will tell you he is all the time, Boss was correct in the pairing. You and I, we're not different, I suppose. But he has put us together in a different way. He wished for me to be your friend and you mine first. All the other urges, such as sex, have been put on the back fire."

"Burner. What do you mean, all the other urges? And sex?" Tholan told her. "So, once the two mates come together, they're horny for each other to the point where they might have sex within like, minutes of meeting."

"I can only guess what the word horny is, but if it is as I think, then yes, they are very horny for each other. But there is also a great deal of fighting." She asked him when he'd found out about this, and not to dismiss a fight. "No, I will not. But I only found out about it when we were in the living room of Riss. After your dream. Michael told me."

She stood there for several seconds. Then a minute of pacing. When she stopped and looked around, Parker thought that this was as good as any place for a fight and yelled for Michael and Boss to come to her now. When they both appeared in her room, she drew the sword that had been given to her and pointed it at Michael's heart.

"Which one of you will die if I don't get some answers right now?"

71

Chapter 5

Boss had nearly burst out laughing several times already. The woman was just as he'd thought she'd be. Loving, and mean when pushed. And right now, Michael was pressed up against the wall of her room begging for help from him. Boss might have helped but he was dangerously close to laughing, and he was afraid she'd turn the sword on him. But it was Tholan who cooled her temper.

"I do not believe you can kill him. You might nick him a few times, but—"

Michael cut Tholan off before he could continue. "Tholan, you are not helping me. Please do not tell her those things. I should like to be unharmed when I return to the other realm." Michael looked at Boss. "Will you stop laughing for two seconds and come here and talk to Parker? She might do more than nick me, and then turn on you."

"She cannot, and this you are aware of." Boss laughed out loud now. "Parker dear, if you were to put away the sword for a moment or two, I shall answer any and all questions that you have. Oh, before I forget to tell you, the demon is free to

73

continue with his plans for now. I have a plan that will benefit you more than you can imagine."

"Well, aren't you a wealth of not good information. And with this guy, I don't know. I can imagine a great many things to do to him. Like having him tied up by one leg hanging from the nearest tree like a fucking pinata. He might not have candy in him, but I'm sure that it would be just as delightful for me to bang him around for a few days." Boss laughed harder. He wasn't sure if it was from the look on Michael's face or what Parker had said. "Then there is you. What if I stuck you over a pit and roasted your ass for a while? Do you think you'd be tender?"

"Nay, I would not." He snapped his fingers and Michael was returned to his realm and her sword was put away. The pouty look on Parker's face nearly had him doubling over again, but this was serious, and he needed to calm the young lady. Then the most incredible thing happened.

Tholan took Parker into his arms and held her while she cried. It wasn't anything that he had expected—hoped for, yes, but not expected this soon. He had thought that they'd take their relationship slowly, the two of them getting to know each other, but their attraction for each other had gone beyond what he'd stipulated with his powers; they were already a couple.

"Don't you think I've had enough stress? I've only just gotten out of prison, and my stepmother has turned me over to a demon, who thinks it's his life's work to annoy the shit out of me. You turn up at the strangest times, and you took away my plaything." She glared at him. "You had better do some explaining, or I'm going to find me something else to hurt you with."

"I wanted you to be safe. I have thought of Tholan as

your mate for a good many decades. I thought him to need someone like you in his life. Someone that doesn't pull back when necessary. A woman that would take him to task should he need it, but who could also be soft when needed. And you have both done that." Parker pointed out that Tholan was right there. "Yes, I think that he should hear this as well. But the two of you, you have gotten to the point in your relationship that should have been decades away. Or at the very least after you have become partners in all ways." She asked him what in all ways meant. "Sex. And in love."

"I don't understand this. You picked him out for me, or whatever, decades ago? Before prison?" Boss told her that it had been before she was born. "That's not...I guess it is possible, but why me? And none of this bullshit about me being someone strong. In the event you didn't notice, I'm about as far from strong as a turtle on his back."

"You are much stronger than you give yourself credit for. Both of you. You just needed the right person to bring it out of you. And you have for each other, beyond what I thought was possible." He smiled at them both, and he could see that Parker was getting her dander up. If that saying was apt for someone, it was her. "If you would see your way to it, I would like to marry the two of you right now. It would go a long way in making you safer, Parker. And I think that Tholan would feel better if he could stay here, rather than lurk outside your house."

"I do not lurk. I was simply making sure that nothing untoward was coming for her. That stepmother, she is going to be causing us all trouble, and I do believe that you know it. Of all the things to say to me. I do not lurk." Boss nearly laughed again; the man was as indignant as he'd ever heard him. "And only should she want to marry a man such as me will your services be required."

"What sort of man do you think you are?" Boss was curious about this as well and waited for an answer. "I mean, I'm not going to marry anyone, but why do you think that you're—I don't know, less than someone else?"

"You think me foolish." Parker cocked a brow at Tholan and put her hand on her hip. "I think me foolish then. You could do much better, I think. I'm a protector who has messed up terribly, and—"

"We are not going to go over that again. I have told you, Tholan, everything worked out well. And even though at the time I was mightily upset, I am no longer, and I do not think that you should—"

"Hush." Boss was taken aback. He didn't think anyone had ever told him to hush before. "What did you do, Tholan? I'm sure that whatever it was, you've paid your price. And if you will remember, I'm just coming out of prison myself. I might not have done anything to warrant it, but I was there because the law sent me. And how does society see me right now? An ex-con with a great deal of shit going on. Whatever you've done, I'm sure, as mouthy over there said, you've more than paid the price for your actions."

"I took a woman too soon." Boss held his breath. He didn't want this brought up now. Perhaps never, but he said nothing as Tholan continued. "She was hurt, and I thought her dead. But in the end, her life, that of the man she was to marry, generations of children that might have been born to her, were wiped out. Her mate, the one set to marry her, had no one to love in his life. It was something that I have thought about my entire life since then. You have nothing to be ashamed about that has happened to you. You were just a spawn in all this."

"Pawn. And I was. But as I said, that doesn't mean much to some people." Parker turned and looked at Boss. "You set us up to come together. I have no reason to think that you've made a mistake, but if you would please explain to me how this will benefit us both, then I'm willing to listen. Tholan has come to mean a great deal to me. And while I'm not sure that I love him, I'm sure that I could be happy being with him for the rest of my life."

"You're immortal." Parker said nothing but looked at Tholan. "He didn't know. And I swear to you, Parker, it was my intention to tell you, but with this demon and you seeing him, it has thrown my plans and thoughts off a bit. As I told you before, I cannot see things going on in the other world. But as soon as you told me what you knew, I made sure that I got as much information that I could. And I have it."

"So, I'm immortal. What does that have to do with this? I'm assuming something is about to occur and you want...I have no idea what you want, but I'm betting that it has something to do with what you've found out." He nodded and glanced at Tholan. "Does he know?"

"No, not as yet. It is why I came here, to tell you what I knew, ask that you marry him, and to get a look at the piece that you have of him. And please, do not say his name aloud. You have contact with the others in the group now, all of them. So, if you must mention his name, say so with that link." Parker told him that she could do that. She went to the floor and pulled up the rug there. "If you were to allow me to simply put my hand on that device, I can see into it. You do not have to open it for me."

When he put his hand on the unopened safe, he saw what he'd been asking about. He also saw that the letter from her father, as well as other items, were still in the safe, some of them yet untouched. He wondered if she was waiting or if she'd simply missed them. Moving the items more out in the open, he took his hand away and nodded to her. They made their way to the living room, where Maggie was there waiting.

"Miss, I didn't know you had company. I should like to speak to you when you are free. It is...it's important." When Maggie put the thick envelope in her pocket, Boss sent a little more strength her way. Maggie would do this and make the household better for it. "I shall bring in some scones, warm from the oven, and tea then."

Before anyone could answer her, she left. Boss looked at Parker. She was thinking hard on what to do. It was in her nature to hit things straight on, but in this, it was better that Maggie come to her. Things, he knew, were never as easy as they seemed. Nor as difficult for one person as they might be for someone else. It would work out, this he knew.

"As I have said, I should like to have you wed. Being done by my hand will give you so much more than you both have now. And in dealing with this particular demon, you will need the strength of this as well as the rest of the Mystics. I have it on good authority that you will have your license to practice law reinstated should your sentence for the crimes that you did not commit be removed. Is that true?" Parker was lost in thought and he asked her again. "Is it true then? You could become an attorney as you should have been all along?"

"Yes. I guess. I'm not sure that I'd be any good at it anymore." Tholan asked her why not. Boss wanted to know was well, although he could guess. "I've been to prison. I know how they are treated, the inmates. And a great many of them profess to be innocent. While I'm not stupid enough to think that they all are, I do think that a great many of them are in there because of bad representation. I was actually thinking that I'd like to help with the charities and such that are going on around town. I certainly have enough to keep me busy for a while."

"I have a great deal of money as well. We all do. I do not know if I'd still be getting paid or not, but I'd enjoy you using it for good as well." Boss said that they'd both be paid, a goodly sum too. "There, see? We have plenty of money for you to help with."

"You both will. And with a license, you'd be able to help with all the paperwork that comes with running charities, as well as corporations such as the one that the others are thinking of opening." He had only heard about the corporation from Michael; it was still being talked about by the others. "Not to mention, you'd keep them out of hot water should it come to that. I know that there are rules in donating money, as well as costs that come with that. I think that you'd be able to help them in all sorts of ways, my dear."

"All right." He looked at Tholan when she spoke. It was him that asked what she was all right with. "All of it. Marriage, licenses if I can get them back, as well as the magic. But I do have two things that I'd like to see happen. There was a woman that was in one of the cells close to mine. I would like to know if she really did kill her family because a demon told her to. Also, the cook at the prison—is she using poison to kill all the inmates off that use catsup? She seemed like she was just a little off—but then, I'm hardly a judge of that."

"Yes, she did kill her family because of a demon. But, as I have said before, I cannot see things in the other world until it's too late. She is happiest there, I think, where the other world demons cannot get to her. It is what kept you safe for all those years." She nodded, then asked about the catsup. "No. Just a nasty rumor that was started before she was incarcerated. It was the previous cook that was poisoning the inmates. But she has been dealt with. I believe that she is being taken care of by the state and is living out a happy life away from the kitchen."

When she seemed satisfied with the answers, he pulled the rings that he'd had made for these two from his pocket. They were getting a great deal more than the others. It was necessary for them to have it. But until she had told him about the demon, he'd not a clue why. Boss decided that he'd be much more diligent from now on about his plans.

Taking their hands into his larger ones, he looked at them both. They were in love, just the beginnings of it, and Boss thought that he might well enjoy watching it blossom between them. The rest of them had come together hard. Their anger at each other was also fun, but this was something that he would enjoy more. Romance was a beautiful thing, and he was so glad that it had been something that he'd figured out long ago.

"These rings are made of my love for the two of you. Magic to keep you safe, and a bit of myself so that others, otherworld creatures, will know that not only are you mine, but that you will forever be in my heart." He kissed their cheeks and gave a bit more of himself to them before continuing. "Forever will your hearts be one. Your children will be safe as well. Anything and everything you do, it will be for the good of the world. And no one could ask for two better people to do that than the couple before me."

Tholan was shy, but then so was Parker for all her troubles. So when they only touched their lips to each other's cheeks, Boss took away the hold that he had on them and stepped back. They would be stronger than anyone that he'd ever created before, and they would need to be.

"Now, I should be going. I have a great many things to do between now and forever." He laughed and was happy that they did as well. "I think that you should go to the compound and let them know what has happened today. I love you both."

Going to his office, Boss sat down at his desk. It was easier on him now, the work. It wasn't as hard on him as it had been so many years ago. There were so few people in the world then that Michael and he had been there for each passing. Then it was as if he barely had time for doing what needed to be done. Now, even though it was still stressful at times, he was getting more done, and he was getting out of the office more. That, to him, was the best of the best.

~*~

Parker went to the kitchen with Tholan. She had to talk to Maggie anyway, and thought this was as good a time as any to tell her what she knew. Also, she wanted to be able to tell someone that she was married, and Maggie, while she was in trouble, would be the best for her to talk to about it. As they sat at the kitchen table, Maggie pushed a thick envelope at her.

"Before you were arrested, Mr. March came to my husband and I and, uh—told us that we were to get a cut in pay. That the household was spending too much, and since we lived on the grounds in the cook's house, we shouldn't have as many bills as the rest, but we did. We had our own power and water bills like the house did. And we didn't order our food with the household. We did our own shopping." Parker opened the envelope and looked at the paycheck stubs that were in it. She was stunned to see how much they had been cut. "We didn't have the funds to even feed ourselves after that. It was as if — well, we thought your father was punishing us for something, and we were to speak to him the morning after he was arrested."

"How long? When was it that Mr. March cut your pay?" She knew but wanted to know it from Maggie as well. "Six years. He took half your check for six years. I wish you'd have come to us, Maggie. This is not what my dad would have done, and I know that he didn't order this."

"We took food." Parker nodded. "And a little of the petty cash when we were going to get our power cut off. I know that we live in the house, but there were expenses too. When I'd try to tell your father about the stove that went out or the furnace that had stopped working, Mr. March said that he'd handle it."

Maggie started to cry, and Parker took her hand in hers. It was almost scary to see how much she had suffered; how cold they'd been living back there until the weather turned. She decided right then and there if Mr. March weren't already dead, she'd kill him herself. There was more too, things that Maggie wasn't going to bring up, but Parker pushed her, not sure if it worked until she started talking again.

"My Lanny, he got sick that year. The cold was too much for him, and I nearly lost him. Had it not been for the insurance that was provided, I don't know what would have happened to him. We'd hide in the house on the coldest nights…to keep warm, you see. I felt horrible about it, knowing that the mister was only trying to save money. But when Mrs. Brooks came into the house with new shopping bags filled with things that I'd have to wash and iron for her, it made it hard for us to want to stay around. Then I heard that you were in prison, that you'd done it for your daddy. And that was when we decided to stay. After Mr. March passed, our checks were the same as they'd been before. We've been putting the things back that we took. The list of the food and other things are there as well, and how much we have paid back. It's not a lot, I'm sorry to say, but we've had to catch up on our other bills or be tossed out."

"I'm so sorry. Sorrier than I could ever tell you." She looked at Tholan and he nodded, just like he knew what she was thinking. Perhaps he did. "I'm going to have Allen look into this. And there will be no more of you paying us back for this either. I'm just so glad that you stayed for me and my da. This will be fixed, Maggie, and I'm so very sorry that it happened to you. To the nicest people that I know. But I'd like to tell you something — you'll be the first to know. Tholan is my husband."

"Oh my." Maggie got up and danced around the kitchen, which made them both laugh. "This is the grandest news. Your father, he'd be so happy about this that I'd bet that he'd be busting buttons that I'd have to put back on his suit for him. Oh, my child, I'm so glad to see you married. What is your married name now?"

Parker didn't know. Tholan had told her that he didn't have one; a last name was something that he'd not needed and hadn't gotten one. But he smiled at her, then at Maggie, as he stood up to hug their cook.

"We're Mr. and Mrs. Tholan Daniels." Parker looked at him when Maggie made the connection. "Yes, just like her father's middle name. It was set to be, and I could not be a happier man because she is in my life."

Parker loved it as well. But then Tholan did something that she wasn't sure why. He asked that Maggie not tell anyone as yet; they wanted to surprise a few people when the time was right. Meggie nodded. She did ask if she could tell her husband, and they both nodded. Parker asked him about that when they got into the car to head to the compound.

"I have an idea why Boss has done this that will help the two of us. The demon, he knows your name, you told me." She nodded. "You are no longer that person. If he does not know your true name, which I was to tell you the paperwork has been put in the court building, then he cannot claim what is not his to take."

"It's county courthouse, and is that all it takes?" Tholan said that it was not, but it was a start. "I have to get in touch with Allen. He'll have to figure out what sort of other things March did to our staff. Not that there are many of them left—I think I know why now—but it's not right that he did that."

"I believe that he was working with your stepmother. Perhaps he was funding her for things that she would need after your father passed. I do not know all the details of their relationship, but it was one that was as loving as it was volatile. Your stepmother, she has a temper that scares me."

"Did she kill my father? I need to know that. I probably don't really want to know, but I need to know." He said that she did not. "Thank you for that. I don't know what I would have done had she had anything to do with his death. It's hard enough on me that he's gone, and I wasn't there for him."

"But you were." She looked at him as he smiled at her. "Your father had many pictures of you around him when he passed. Some of them when you were very young. I believe I was told that there were many of the two of you together. One that was particularly close to him was the one of the day you were born. He held you in his arms and told you of all the things that you were to do together. And he did all of them and more because he loved spending time with his precious little girl. That was what he called you, was it not? Then there

84

were films of you on the screen in his room all the time, the sound just loud enough for him to hear. His protector is now at the compound should you like to speak to him. But he told me that your father loved you more than he'd ever seen a man love his child. He said that it was what made his passing so much easier for him, that you were surrounding him when he closed his eyes for the final time."

"Oh Tholan, thank you for that. I didn't know. He...I loved him with all that I had to give to someone. And I think—just now I realized that I love you just as much." He kissed her on the cheek, and she smiled at him when he took her hand. "I believe us being married would have made him happy. Just as Maggie said, he would have popped buttons."

"I think she needs more help. I have not used a staff before, but I think that she needs help around that house of yours." Parker told him it was their home. "Yes, thank you for that. I do have a great deal of money. I have had to invest a great deal of it so that I wouldn't have it all in one place. Something about eggs and baskets. I didn't understand, but I was told that it was a good thing."

"Putting all your money in one place, like in a single investment or bank, is a bad idea because there is the off chance that the company could fail you. If you have your money spread around, as I do too, then if something happens in one place, you still have funds to fall back on. If you don't mind me asking, how much do you have." He told her, and she asked if he was serious.

"I have no sense of humor, or so I have been told. Is ninety billion a great deal? I have had no use for money from working. I recently purchased a home, but it is very small in comparison to your...our home now. I believe I could fit the one I bought into your living room and have room still left over." They were laughing as the limo pulled up on front of the compound. "Remember what Boss said about the demon. I would also tell them our name the same way. They will have heard about your troubles, so they will not be surprised about the secrecy."

She understood the name thing now. The demon had called her by her full name several times. What she didn't understand and would ask about when she was on safe grounds, was why that mattered. And for that matter, how had Angela been able to do such a thing? She knew why—the bounty that she got from it would give her immortality. Perhaps, Parker thought, she should have asked for good health as well. Parker asked Tholan about that.

"You will never be ill. Never suffer in ways that will harm you or any children that are brought into our home. Nor will you age or gain weight." She asked about children. "Sadly, because of what I am, I cannot give you a child of my own. But if you would agree, as the others have done, we can take in as many or as few as you wish. They will be better off with us, I think, as we have a great deal to offer them."

"But we won't give them everything. My da said that to give a child whatever they want would spoil the adult when they grew up. I worked for whatever I wanted. He helped me with college and books, but he didn't give me anything extra while away." Tholan said that was a wonderful idea. "Yes, my da, he was a very good man, and had a good head on his shoulders."

"As do you." They got out of the limo and she could feel the magic right away. Her back tingled a bit, and she thought that it was the magic. Tholan laughed. "I forgot to mention that you have wings as well. Here, you can pull them out should you wish, and be safe. I cannot wait to see you in all your glory, my wife. You have made me the happiest man alive, and I love you with all my heart."

She was in love with a man that loved her, and she'd have the rest of her life to show him what he'd given her in the way of his heart. Parker didn't know what was in store for her in the future, but she knew that whatever it was, she'd be able to deal with it much better now that Tholan was beside her.

Chapter 6

Angela paced her living room. It was so small all she was able to put in it was a couch plus a small table for her lamp. And even that was taking up too much room. She glared at the small television set that she'd gotten on sale two weeks ago. Money hadn't been a problem for her in a very long time, and now it was all she could think about. How she was going to pay for everything seemed to be all she could think about these days.

Shopping had been her pastime. Fucking someone too, but shopping had given her more pleasure than most men could. Shoes were her fetish. Dresses of every color under the rainbow were another thing that she just could not get enough of. Angela didn't even care if they fit or that she would never wear them. It was owning them that had given her what she needed. And now that was all gone as well. And when she'd been tossed, literally tossed, from her home, she'd not been able to take more than what she had on with her when turned away.

"That fucking girl did this to me. Why did she have to

89

confess to the crimes that weren't hers to take on?" Well, neither were they Parker's, the late, and her asshole of a husband, but that was neither here nor there. "He was to go to prison, I was going to have the will he had made up changed because of his guilt, and then I'd be on easy street. But no, that fucking girl. She was forever doing shit like this to me."

There were several times that Angela was sure that Parker knew what she was about. Then after his death, she'd found out that not only had he known, but he'd thought it funny. Her taking the credit cards that were so generously given to her and buying anything that she wanted, then two weeks later taking it all back for the cash. It had served her well over the years, but that had been cut off when Joey died. Joey March had been her savior. Not her love—no, she didn't love him at all—but he had provided her with money, going so far as to steal it from the servants when she asked for more.

"Oh, but to be able to go there and thank Maggie for all her suffering so that all her hard-earned money went for me to have my breasts redone, my legs to look good in heels, and for my face to look twenty years younger." She glanced at the mirror that had been covered up recently. "What the hell was that guy thinking when he told me that I would be beautiful forever?"

"I said no such thing." When he appeared in the room, the demon that she'd made the deal with, Angela fell back on the couch. "You are looking your years, Angela Brooks. Whatever have you done with yourself?"

"This is all your fault. I told you that I didn't want to get fat. And look at me." She shook the pouch that was her belly and glared at him. "You lied to me."

"No. You said that you didn't want to gain weight, and you haven't—not a single ounce. It's not my problem that you have gone to pot. You should more than likely get out more and walk. I'm to understand that would help you. However, I'd not count on it. You did make a deal with a demon, did you not?"

Growling at him, she knew better than to leap at him. The man was scary, and the fact that he could change at will frightened her even more. The last time she'd tried that, he'd changed into a large spider and had stabbed her over and over until she finally passed out.

"When are you going to take her? I thought once she was released you could just take her with you, and I'd be able to take over my home again." Angela looked around the room that she was in. "I'm sick of living in this dump."

"Yes, I do see where you have come down in the world of money. But if you were to ask me, I believe that this is just where you belong. Someone who would sell their own daughter deserves no less than this. Well, perhaps less, but that is not my job." She asked him what his job was. "To collect and deliver the dead that belong there to Hell. And in answer to your question, I cannot take her as yet. She has something of mine, and until I get it, I have to wait. Your daughter has been very naughty, I think. I have been looking, but in the last few days, I have been barred even from her home."

"It's my home. And I want to get it back." Angela wasn't sure how she was going to make that happen. The stupid chit had more than likely made out a will, as her father had done, making it so that she got nothing from the estate and could never buy the family home. Christ, what a nightmare this had been. "She's living it up while I have nothing. I should have bargained for money too."

"I do not have access to funds, I'm afraid. Not for you, at any rate. But she is giving away a great deal, did you know that? Charities for the poor and stupid. I do hate those things. They give people hope, and with hope comes enlightenment. Both of which I have no control over." Angela said nothing, not even sure why he cared if they were given hope. "You will understand soon enough. I wish for you to sneak into the home for me. There is something, as I have mentioned, that belongs to me there. If you find it for me, bring it to me soon, then I shall make sure that you have enough funds to live out your life, as well take the girl with me. Without it, I cannot do a thing."

"This piece, what is it exactly? I need to know what to look for, don't I?" He showed her his hand; the upper half, where his fingers would have joined this palm, was missing. "How the hell did she do that?"

"Precisely. If you find it in a timely manner, then I will give you rewards that will help you in this life you have asked for, as well as put you in a position where you no longer have to worry about food coming in or where you are living. That will change much as well." He put out his hand and she hesitated. "It's up to you, Angela Brooks. I care not if you work for me or not. There are others that I could call —"

"No, I'll do it." She put her hand into his and felt the power and heat of him. The searing pain of it had her dropping to the floor and she screamed. "Let me go. Please, I beg you, let me go."

When he released her, the man disappeared. Angela laid on the floor, holding her injured hand cupped into the other. She couldn't even look at it — she just knew that he'd seared it off at the wrist. Getting up, staggering slightly, she made her way to the kitchen area, holding onto whatever was close to her to keep herself upright.

Running the tap on cold, she waited until she knew the

water was cold enough to take off the heat before she chanced a glance at her hand. There didn't seem to be anything on it, just a small mark in the palm of her hand. When the water cooled it off as best as she could feel, Angela sat down at her makeshift table and studied the mark that the demon had left on her.

It was too hard to make out, the thing was so small. Getting up, feeling weak in not just her legs but her back as well, she made her way to her desk and pulled out her magnifying glass—another thing that she'd had to resort to when the fucking man had done this to her.

Looking at the mark she could just make out the first letter, and it looked like a "W." The second letter, if that was what it was, had been marked through with a pointed line. It took her all of ten minutes to figure out that it was the tail of the devil. Then the other letter made itself known to her. It was a pitchfork, one like she'd seen in pictures depicting the devil himself.

Looking around, trying to imagine what sort of things that he was up to now, she asked the empty room what it meant. If she had expected an answer, Angela might have been more prepared for the being that joined her in the room. But he was looming over her, his big body shifting into that of a man just as she was ready to scream.

Her clothing was burnt off her, and she lay naked before the person. And when he rammed his cock into her pussy, heating her to the point that Angela thought she was being cooked from the inside out, she screamed out a release that made her dizzy. Whatever he was doing to her besides giving her the best fuck of her life, she liked it, even if he was killing her with the fire between her thighs.

"Do not speak." Nodding as he took her up and over

the pinnacle again, Angela felt his fiery mouth at her throat, then at her breast. As soon as he suckled her, his tongue making her nipple feel as if it were being torn from her, she came again and again until she was weak from it. And when he finished with her, filling her body with his molten cum, Angela screamed again, her body on fire, quite literally.

Looking down at herself, she saw the blisters all over her tender, reddened skin. Large and full of puss, they seemed to move when she did, jiggling in a way that made her sick to her belly. Her left breast hurt the most, and she was afraid that it would fall off her body should she move. He sat there on the other side of her, on the couch, and smoked a cigar with his naked body there for her to see. His cock, thick and still hard, dripped a dark red gooey substance that she thought might be lava. Angela looked at him when he said her name.

"You are marked for me. I will have you like this whenever I wish. You may speak to me now." She asked him who he was. "You may call me Merlin. I have taken you from Rollin."

"I don't know a Rollin, and if Parker sold me to you, I want to know why. She fucking has everything." He grinned at her and the cigar disappeared. When he began to stroke his cock, she felt her mouth water. "I can't move and you fucking know it. You have hurt me badly with your fucking sex."

"You have enjoyed me too. I should like for you to suck me off. I will reward you greatly if you please me." Angela was pulled up from her position on the couch and her head shoved to his cock. "Do not think of biting me, for if you do, then I shall do the same to you. But believe me when I tell you, my bite to your tender skin will hurt thousands of times worse than you can do to me."

Angela had no choice but to take him into her mouth. He was too large, his cock cutting off the air to her lungs when he shoved her head up and down over him. All she wanted to do was go to the shower and try and cool herself off. Then as suddenly as she thought of the pain, she was healed.

"I have given you relief for now. And you will have something to help you enjoy what we're doing. But do not expect this every time." The cock slid into her pussy was thick, but not nearly as much as the one she had in her mouth. "This is a pleasure bitch. She has a cock to please you with, or a pussy should you want to taste her. She is not hot, but she can give you incredible pleasure, when I have had mine. Now, see to my needs."

The cock in her pussy was making her insane with the need to come. And in turn, she decided to get Merlin off so that she could have her fun as well. Cupping his hot balls into her hand, Angela felt the cum there, the fullness of him. And when she gave them a small twist, he pushed her head harder down over him as he filled her with his hot cum once again. The pleasure bitch bit her on the shoulder and Angela came so hard that she passed out from it.

When she woke, after only a few minutes, she thought, the bitch was sitting on Merlin's cock, riding him like he was a big bull. When Angela noticed her cock too, seeping at the tip, red with the blood that was there, she leaned over and took it into her mouth. The hand entering her pussy had her riding the fingers of the woman. Angela was in heaven, she thought.

All of a sudden, she found herself hurling across the room, her body slammed against the wall so hard that she could feel all the bones that had been broken. Not able to move with the lamp parts that had been broken holding her upright, she looked at Merlin when he thundered his way to her.

"You will not have such thoughts again." The slap took

her breath away, which was good, she supposed, since she was finding it difficult to breath. "What the fuck were you doing? Are you trying to piss me off? And I was going to give myself of you again. Nay, not now, I shan't. Never think those thoughts again! Do you hear me?"

The next slap knocked her out. Angela knew that she was going to die, that she was going to be found burned and blistered, her body broken and held up by the ugliest lamp that she'd ever seen. Merlin drew back again, like she'd not done what he'd asked. So she did the only thing she could think of; she begged.

"I'm so sorry. Please, don't hit me again. I'm going to die as it is." He pointed out that she'd been made an immortal by Warrior, but with stipulations. "Yes, well, I'm going to spend the rest of my days broken and bleeding here if you hit me again. I beg of you, give me another chance. I won't think or say those thoughts again. I promise you, but please, don't hit me."

He did hit her, his fist as big as her head. And Angela, already broken badly, let darkness take her. And she was going to do her damnest to figure out what she'd thought so that she'd never ever think that again. Whatever it was, it was no longer going to be a thought that she would have.

~*~

Tholan looked over the paperwork that had been handed to him. He could read it but understanding what he was looking at was making his head ache. Ready to tell the man in front of him that he'd be back, Judith came into the room with him and smiled.

"I'm very sorry, Tholan. I should have been on time. But you know how it is when you're making jam. There is no time to waste when it's ready." Tholan nodded but was clueless as to what she was talking about, or what she was doing here. "I'm here to help Mr. Daniels in this transition. His wife sent me here with the instructions that I was to give him anything that he needed. You may call her if you wish."

"No, no. That won't be necessary. She's already called in and told my secretary that you were running late. To be honest, Judith, I'm not sure what you're doing here either." She explained it to him. "Oh, well, that makes perfect sense. Then I will start over. These are papers that will give him access to all the money, property, and any future endeavors that Ms. Brooks has."

As he droned on, Judith told Tholan why she was really there. It wasn't to help the banker with the paperwork that would also make it so that Parker had access to his money, but to help him understand where to sign.

It was making no sense to me. I think he thought that I should know some of the terms he was using. I was in over my head, I think. Judith said that it was a lot to take in. *Yes. Or it could be that I should have done what the others have said to me and come to this realm more often. Things that are said, the double meaning of some of the words, they really are hard to keep straight, aren't they?*

Sometimes. But I'm here to make sure that you know where to sign or not. And I've looked into this man's mind. He is someone that we can trust. Tholan nodded and signed his new name to the pages where he was told. Tholan Daniels wasn't that hard of a name to remember, but he'd had to practice writing it over and over at home before coming here. *Parker said that you didn't know how to sign your name. That's not really that uncommon, Tholan. I don't even think they're teaching cursive in school anymore. You're doing a fantastic job.*

He hoped so. It was important to him not to embarrass Parker, or any of the rest of them. When it was his turn to sign the paperwork for Parker to use his money and other items that he'd invested in, it was much easier. Tholan didn't even have to think about his name now; it flowed from his mind as easily as it did from the pen.

It took them almost an hour to finish his end of the work. Then he had to go by the social security office and pick up his new card; his credit cards, he'd been assured, would be ready by the time he returned. And then he was going to go to the compound and work with some of the new protectors on scheduling. He was being replaced by a team of men. That made him feel better, knowing that it would take more than one person to continue his work the way he'd been doing it. Boss was waiting in his new office when Tholan entered.

"I have good news for you. I'm to understand that you have been given this office, correct?" Tholan nodded and ran his hands over his new desk. It was twice as big as the one that he'd had before. "The good news. I have hired two people to come in and redo the offices where you were working. I hadn't realized that it had become so dated. You're a good man for doing that job for so long without complaint."

"You would have told me to suck it up or something like that." Boss laughed with him. "Parker is very good at correcting me. She just tells me what I should have said and goes on as if it doesn't happen hourly. But I love her, and that makes it easier to mess up. There are times when I find myself thinking of something wrong just to have her smile at me. What else have you to tell me?"

"The demon that wants Parker has marked her stepmother for Merlin." Tholan was glad that he was seated, otherwise he was sure that he would have fallen down. "Yes, I knew you'd remember him. Merlin laid claim to Angela just yesterday, in a most horrific way. She will heal, no doubt, but she will not do so quickly nor easily the way that he is abusing her."

"Does Parker know?" He shook his head. "Are you wanting me to tell her, or are you wishing to do so? I will, should you wish, but Parker was in such a good mood this morn, I'd hate to snow on her dance party."

"That's a good one. You will need to say that to Parker. But in answer to your question, no, I don't want her to know right now. It would do her no good as she cannot help her, nor do I think she would. But it would upset her needlessly to know that she is being hurt." Tholan shook his head. "You think that she would wish to know?"

"No, I think she should be told regardless. It might be the woman that caused her harm, but I don't believe that it is up to us to not let her make that decision on her own. Parker might not care a fig, but she will need to be told." Boss nodded at him, then smiled. "You have something else in mind?"

"No, I just never thought I'd say this to you, but you're a much better man than even I am. I would have not told her simply because I would not want to...I think that they call it deal with it. But you're absolutely right. It's not our business to make that decision for her. Good man, Tholan, Parker is a very lucky young woman to have a man like you in her life."

"I believe that it is I that am lucky. I have her in my life and I feel settled. Loved. I never thought that I'd be loved like this. It's a good feeling." Boss told him that he loved him. "Yes, but you aren't Parker, nor a woman."

"Very true. Also, I'd like for you both to be there when I have to go and talk to the king of the other world. Something needs to be done about this bargaining thing they have going on. I realize that this one with Parker has been going on for some time, but this is ridiculous, don't you think?" He said that it was. "I should get going. But I will tell you two when

I have it set up. He's a good man, other than the fact that he's my opposite, so I foresee no issues. Oh, and I'll need for Parker to bring the piece that she has of this demon. That way, if he asks for it, we'll be ready."

"I'll ask her." Boss nodded again as he stood up. "I do have a question for you, Boss. You can not answer me if you wish, but it's been weighing heavily on my mind the last couple of days. Is Parker a descendent of my charge?"

Boss was shocked but sat back down. He didn't say anything for a long few moments; the time seemed to stretch out for an eternity. And when he nodded, Tholan let out a breath that he felt he'd been holding for years instead of only a few seconds.

"Even though she'd been paralyzed, she managed to have a child. But she adopted so many more. They were happy, these children that came to mean as much to her as her own blood had. They went on to be happy adults, as well as men and woman that made a difference in the world." With a wave of his hand Boss brought up the face of the woman that Tholan had thought himself in love with. "She wasn't in love with her husband, not like you are with Parker, but she was happy. The children gave her peace, as well as filled a place in her heart that no one could touch but them. Parker is a very distant grandchild of her biological daughter. A single daughter was born of the women every generation. Sadly, your Parker will be the last. It is only fitting that you, of all people, get to see her happier than her ancestor would have ever been, I think, with the mate that had been for her."

"As a punishment." Boss told him no, never that. "Then why would you pick someone for me whose ancestor I killed?"

"You did no such thing, Tholan. You made a mistake, one that you have paid for many times over. Parker is her

100

own person, nothing at all like your charge. And I have to admit, I think she turned out to be a better person than I could have hoped for. She is with you because I wanted you to see that mistakes happen, but sometimes good comes from them. Like the goodness of Parker's mother. And her mother before her. Parker is also a good person, a wonderful mate to you. A woman that will raise children with you that will go on to be happier still than the two of you. You might have messed up a single thing in her life, one tiny thing that did change the world around her, but it was only Beth's world, not that of her offspring."

"I love her, Boss. With all that I am." Boss told him that was as it should be. "We have talked about children, about our lives."

"But you have not slept with her." Tholan shook his head, lowering his eyes so that Boss could not see the shame in his statement to him. "Tholan, look at me. You and Parker have a long life to live, longer than anyone that she knows. Sex is not everything in a relationship. It's good for it, will strengthen your love, but it's not a make or break deal in keeping two together. You will get to it when you do. And until then, you're becoming close. Friends, the friends that I wanted you to be before you fell in love. This too is working out better than I could have hoped for. As I have said before, you and Parker are stronger than all the others put together with the amount of love that you have. And your powers, when they are needed, will conquer the world if necessary."

Tholan sat at his desk until darkness made him realize how late it had gotten. Moving to the door, he reached out to Parker to tell her how sorry he was that he'd not come home earlier. She told him that she was working too and hadn't realized what the time was until he contacted her. They decided to meet for dinner in town.

I have a surprise for you. He smiled. This was the third surprise that she'd gotten him this week. *Well, it's for us both. I got us a hot tub. And by the time we get home, it will be ready for us to use.*

Tholan told her that he was excited about that but hadn't a clue why anyone would want a hot tub. He could see where it would keep the bath water warmer, but how would one get into it if the container was too hot? And how did you regulate it so that it didn't burn through the floor? This was the sort of thing that he'd keep to himself. Then when he was shown whatever it was, he'd understand better. But a hot tub? It did not even come to mind how that would be exciting to anyone. Especially since he and Parker only took showers.

Chapter 7

Heather sat huddled in the cell where she'd been put hours ago. The toilet was close to her, but she refused to use it. Anyone could see her, and she wasn't keen on having a bunch of men, even though they were policemen, see her peeing. When the woman who had brought her in came with a pizza box, Heather tightened her grip on herself and tried to make herself as small as possible.

"I can take you to the bathroom that we use if you wish." Hope, a fragile thing, came and went that quickly. "I don't like peeing where people can see me either. And when you've used the bathroom and washed up a bit, you and I are going to share this pizza."

Shaking her head, she watched the woman as she put the box in one hand and opened the door. The door hadn't been locked — she'd told her that when they'd put her in here — but Heather wouldn't try to run. That would get her hurt faster than anything that she'd done before.

The box was set on the bench she was sitting on. Officer Raye sat down beside her too, and Heather whimpered.

103

Moving away, Heather felt better, but she still watched the woman with both eyes open.

"They did a number on you, didn't they? I have been looking for them." Heather jumped up and started for the open door. "I'm going to arrest them, honey, not give you back to them. They'll never touch you again. I will kill them both and go to prison before I ever let them touch you again. Please, have a seat, okay?"

Sitting down again, Heather eyed the pizza. She could smell it. When her belly growled loudly, she looked at the officer to see if she was going to slap her for it. Her father would have. Hell, he'd have hit her several times already while he feasted on the pie. Heather watched as Raye pulled a slice of it out of the box and took a bite of it before handing it to her.

"I don't want you to think that I'd drug you." She'd had that done to her as well. Drugged then left out in the cold while they had their parties. Heather supposed she was lucky that they'd done that rather than leaving her there for anyone to rape. She took a small bite of the pizza and moaned. "It's good, huh? I love a good hot pie. Would you like a soda?"

Nodding, she devoured the slice and held out her plate for another piece. When two more were put on the plate, neither of which had a bite out of them, she ate those while Raye went to get her something to drink. When she returned, Heather was eating the last piece that had been put on her plate, then she sat back. She wasn't full, not even close, but she'd learned the hard way that filling her belly too fast would make her sick.

"I brought you a milk too. Whichever one you wish, there are plenty more in the fridge. They belong to my boss, but Benny won't care. He's coming in later anyway with his wife.

You'll love her. And she is bringing you some cookies and stuff. I bet it's been a while since you've had a hot meal or anything even close to that."

Heather didn't trust the woman, but she was really needing to use the bathroom now. "Can I use your bathroom now?" Raye smiled, and it was almost too much for her to take. No one smiled at her like that, like they really meant it. "Are you really going to hurt them if they come for me?"

"You know it."

They made their way to the ladies' room, and Heather was able to go in by herself. Going to the toilet, she stared at the white thing. Heather hadn't seen a toilet this clean since — well, in forever, she thought.

After relieving herself, Heather washed her hands. She was dirty, she knew that. After spending a week out in the woods, she was bound to be. Washing her face and arms too, she felt reasonably better, but she knew that she needed to have a bath. That was another thing that she'd not had in a while — hot water enough to get herself clean.

Raye was at a desk when she came out, and Heather limped her way back to her cell. The pizza was still there, as well as little cartons of milk, both chocolate and white, as well as several cans of soda. Taking the white milk, she sat there on the floor drinking it as she thought of what had brought her here.

Her parents weren't the best of the lot. Heather thought perhaps she'd been given the worst there was. They were druggies, and they stole things. Even as young as she was, at nine, she knew that it was wrong to go into peoples' houses and take what they had. But that hadn't been the worst of it either. They were also murderers.

Heather was often dragged along on their robberies. They

never asked her to gain access to the houses anymore. Once was enough for her.

The one time, while she'd been having a nice meal with the family, she'd been splattered with their blood. Her father, a big man, had come into the door that she'd unlocked for them and hit the man on the back of the head. The wife, a little elderly woman who had promised her cookies when she was finished eating, was dealt with the same way. Then they made her help carry the things that they'd taken out of the house and into their van. The van that they lived in for the most part.

After that, she'd be made to watch for the police. She did, hoping one of them would do a drive by so that she could flag them down and tell them what was going on. But it never worked out for her, nor the people that lived in the houses.

Then last week, her father had told her that she was going to help them, or else. She didn't know what the "or else" was, but she knew him well enough to know that it could be her death. But the first time they'd made her carry a gun and take it into the house, Heather knew that she couldn't do this. It was just not right. So, taking the gun with her, she ran, and ran for hours before exhaustion took her under.

When she'd woken she'd been in an abandoned barn where the hay smelled sour and the smell of poop made her a little ill. But she'd found some hard corn that wasn't too badly eaten by the rats and made a feast of it. Of course, later she'd been ill, throwing up all over the place then falling asleep again.

Yesterday she'd been looking for something to eat in a dumpster behind the fast food restaurant that had only just recently opened. Heather found some fries and a half-eaten burger, which she cut off the bite marks and devoured. Then she found a can of soda that hadn't been opened, as well as a few more things.

It mattered little to her about dates and expirations because she was so hungry. Heather figured out that the grocery store threw out things with past dates on them every day at opening time. She was eating good until someone caught her.

Heather had been wounded when the man who owned the store shot at her. She kept running until her leg was so sore that she made her way into another unused building. By then her leg was sore to the touch, and she had nothing to clean it with. That was what got her caught this time.

The police officer, Raye, had come upon her when she'd been sobbing as quietly as she could. Her leg was really infected by now, and she was sure that someone was going to come up on her body someday and wonder who she was. Looking up when she heard a sound, Heather was sure that her parents had found her and fought hard not to be taken.

"I have you. Come on, honey, I have you. I'm not going to hurt you." The kindness of her voice had her stopping her fight. Looking at the beautiful woman, she cried harder. "Come on now. I have you. We'll stop by to see a friend of mine, then I'll take you someplace safe. I'm betting that you're Heather Groves, but we won't tell anyone, all right? You'll be safe with me."

The kindness and the fact that her car was cooler than the building had been had Heather falling asleep. When she woke there was a strange man near her, but she couldn't fight him. Someone had tied her to the gurney she was on. But it was his smile — huge, with the whitest teeth she'd ever seen — that calmed her again. With a pinch to her arm, Heather fell asleep again.

He'd stitched her up, Raye had told her. Nineteen of them, and he had cleaned the wound. But she was to go back to the jail so that the man, a Doctor Sheppard, wouldn't be found with her. Her parents, it seemed, were out looking for their daughter, and they were not being nice about it.

And now, here she was in a jail cell with food and a blanket. Heather looked up when someone cleared their throat. The tall man had her moving back from where she was, trying once again to make herself into the smallest ball she could. Once he sat down, she saw something on the man that made her wipe her eyes several times. She could have sworn that the man had wings.

"I'm not going to hurt you, Heather. That is who you are, aren't you?" She nodded at him, and a woman came in. She too had wings, but Heather didn't believe that for a moment. "This is my wife, Lila, and I'm Benny. I wanted to talk to you for a little while, and then I have some friends that would like to take you home. It's a man and wife, and they're about the nicest people you could meet."

"I don't want to be hurt again." Benny said that that would never happen with the Daniels. "Everyone says that, but they do it anyway. I don't want to go back with my mom and dad either. They're not nice people."

"No, they are not. And we're looking for them. Not for you, never that, but to arrest them. They've been killing long enough, don't you think?" Heather said nothing but drank the rest of her milk. "As I was saying, Tholan and Parker, they're coming in to see you. They're good people, as I said, and they're bringing you some shoes. Officer Raye said that she didn't find any when she found you."

"I don't have any." Benny nodded as if he knew that. "They said that you'd bring me cookies. I don't want any, but if I could have them wrapped up, in case this don't work out with those people, I could have myself some food."

"I think it will surprise you how well this will work out with them." Lily handed her a plastic container full of something. Opening it up, Heather looked at the woman again, and her smile brought one out on her own face. "I didn't know what you'd like, so I had Judith make up a variety for you."

Lily asked to look at her leg and Heather let her. It was still very sore, but not as bad as it had been. She couldn't believe that it had only been this morning that the doctor had fixed it. Heather asked if she really had to go with these people. Benny laughed a little before he spoke.

"If you don't like them, we can call someone else in to take you home. It's only to give you a safe place and a shower to use. Food will be plentiful, and I think you're going to love the house. It's really nice." Heather didn't care about houses — she wanted a bath, a soft bed, and no one trying to find her. "Those will come to you as well."

She stared at him and he smiled again. Fear made her stand up, and as she backed her way to the door, she bumped into someone. The arms that picked her up were warm, soft, and full of something that she'd never felt before. Heather had no name for it, but she looked into the eyes of the woman who held her, the man right behind her. They weren't going to harm her. Heather didn't know where that thought had come from, but she believed it. Reaching her fingers up, she ran them over the nose, then the cheeks of the woman.

"You're very soft and clean." She nodded at her, and Heather looked at the man. "Are you going to hurt me? I won't let you if you think to do that."

"Nay, I'd never harm anyone as beautiful and as precious as you are." She believed him. And when he reached for her, she went to him willingly. "We've only just gotten the room done up for you. Well, it was my wife's room when she'd been living in the house once before, but we did get you a new mattress. That was fun. Parker let me bounce on it. I've never done that before."

He was odd but nice, and when Officer Benny said her name, she turned to look at him, tightening her grip on the shirt of the man. Lily handed her the cookies that she'd dropped and kissed her on the cheek. Heather put her hand over the kiss. Something as simple as having people treat her kindly seemed so foreign to her.

"This is Parker and Tholan Daniels. They're the couple that I was telling you about." Benny told them how she'd not wanted to go home with them. "But I think she has since changed her mind. If you guys can handle this, I'll take care of things here, as well as paperwork. Let me know if you have any troubles. I don't think you will, but you'll call if you do."

"We will." She was taken out to a new car. It was one of those kinds that she'd seen in driveways, the kind of car that her father tried to steal all the time. "Once we get home, I'll run a bath for you and see about getting a brush through your hair. It's a pretty color, isn't it?"

Heather didn't know so said nothing. It was just hair as far as she was concerned. The drive to the house was quiet — they didn't turn on the radio to drown her out. Not that she was saying anything, but when their car worked, her father would do that, telling her that if she did talk, he didn't want to hear it.

By the time they pulled up in front of the biggest house she'd ever seen, Heather had worked herself up into fear again. She was in the car with strangers. They were taking her to their house to do whatever they wanted. When the door beside her was opened, it wasn't the couple who had come to get her, but another man, one that she'd seen before.

"I know you." He nodded and put out his hand. "I'm afraid that they'll hurt me. I don't want to go inside."

"They would rather die than to harm you. It will hurt them badly because you have been so neglected. I told you that I was going to keep you safe, did I not?" She nodded. "Then you must believe me once again when I tell you that you will forever be safe here. This I promise you."

"Yes, all right."

She took his hand and like before felt the tingle of something run up her arm. Going into the house, the man was gone, but she knew that he was close to her. He'd been there for her every step of the way to the building she'd been hiding in. Heather stepped into the house and knew that everything that she'd known before had been a lie. This was what a home felt like.

~*~

Tholan sat on the floor outside the bathroom to hear his wife, and hopefully soon to be daughter, speaking. Mostly Parker was telling her how sorry she was about the tangles in her hair and hurting her, and Heather was telling her it was all right. The two of them, it seemed to him, were getting along better than he'd expected. Especially so soon after bringing Heather into their lives.

When the door opened finally, Tholan stood up. He almost didn't recognize the child when she stepped through the doorway and into the hall. She was clean, yes, but it was more than that. He could see freckles on her nose, the slight pink to her cheeks, as well as her lips that were no longer cracked and peeling. Touching his fingers to her hair, he smiled at her.

He got down on his knees to be eye level with her. "I thought that the other little girl had been sucked down the drain and they left us with you. My goodness, you are a pretty little girl, are you not? And freckles. I love freckles on cheeks. Parker has them as well." She hid slightly behind Parker, and he had a feeling that he was scaring her. Backing up, Tholan stood up and walked down the hall to the room that had been Parker's. "As I said before, we got you a new mattress. Tomorrow we will go shopping and find you things that you like."

Tholan hoped that she'd follow him. The pajamas that she had on were too big, so when she entered the room with him, with Parker right behind her, Heather kicked off the bottoms and got onto the big bed. Once she was there, she looked around the room, and neither he nor Parker moved.

"Why would you change it? I don't know that I can stay that long. They said my mom and dad are looking for me." Tholan sat in the chair by the desk and Parker on the bed. "This is a pretty room. You lived here?"

"I did. When I was just a little girl like you. My mom, she passed away when I was born. There was a car accident." Heather nodded. "You're going to be here forever if we can convince you to have us. We're newly married and were talking about children when the call came that you were needing someone to take you. But, as Lily said, if you don't like us or want to go elsewhere, we—"

"No. I mean no, I don't want to go anyplace else. I like this room too." Heather looked around, then back at them. "Don't let them get me. I don't...one time I had to wear the mask of my enemy. They killed this really nice couple that didn't mean anybody any harm. Their blood got all over me. And my mom said that I wasn't to wash it off on account of it being the blood of my enemies."

"That's horrible." Heather nodded at him when he spoke. "That will never happen here. We don't kill...why, I don't believe we even have any enemies, do we, Parker?"

"None that matter." He'd forgotten about the demon and her stepmother. But she was right. None of them mattered, and he'd make sure that she never had a terrible thing like that done to her again. "Now. As we were saying, we will take you tomorrow to get something to wear that fits. We also have an appointment with a doctor. Lily is a good friend of ours, and she's going to give you the okay to register for school. But for now, we have some people, again that we trust, that are going to come here and give you a good education until your parents are found. All right?"

"I don't know anything about school. I mean, I've never been." Tholan wanted to gather Heather up in his arms and hold her until the world understood that this wasn't a way to treat a child. "I know how to read and stuff. And I know most of my numbers to say them, but that's about all I can do. You going to take me back to them?"

"No. Why would you think that? You're ours, Heather. As soon as I saw you and you hugged me, I knew right then that you were our daughter. Isn't that right, Tholan?" He nodded at Parker but watched Heather. "Now, you go to sleep and Tholan and I will be close if you need anything. Our bedroom is at the end of the hallway. I showed you when we came up here, remember?"

"Yes, I remember." Heather laid down and snuggled under the blankets. "This is the softest bed I ever had in my whole life. And I don't want to change the room. I like it just the way it is. Even the dolls."

They left her then, walking hand and hand out into

the hall, but stopped when she asked for the door to be left slightly open.

Parker was crying a little as they made their way to the stairs. Neither of them wanted to leave her, he knew that, but to sit and watch her all night would be unsettling to her. So, they sat on the top step and waited. For what, Tholan wasn't sure, but they weren't going to be far away if she needed them. It was then that Boss showed up.

"If I were to promise you that she will not stir the rest of the night, and that I have Riss watching over her this first night, will you relax and get some rest? She is in the best place possible for her, and for you. Go. Have some fun, and let her protector watch over her."

Tholan knew that if anything were to happen, Riss would protect Heather. He also knew that he'd be close at hand if he needed help. Putting out his hand, Parker took it, but she looked at Boss.

"Will she be ours?" He nodded. "I won't ask you to promise me that. I know that you'd never lie or kid me about something so important to us. Will her parents be dealt with? I don't mean killed, but get what they deserve?"

"What would you think they'd need to be punished? I'm only asking because you said that you didn't mean for them to be killed. What would you like to see happen to them, Parker?" She looked at him, and Tholan told her that he loved her. He, too, would like to see them pay, but he didn't know that death was it. "Let me tell you that they have murdered seven people in the last few years, and all of them have been witnessed by your daughter."

"She told us about the mask. How can people do that to their own flesh and blood?" Tholan knew that it happened all the time. And as protectors, there was little to nothing they could do about it. "I want them to face their crimes."

"They will. I promise." There was something there, something that Boss wasn't saying. Just as he was to ask for clarification, Tholan understood what He wasn't saying.

Yes, he figured, they'd face someone for their crimes. It might not be in a court of law. They might not spend time in a human jail, but they would be judged, and judged for it all. Tholan then remembered that he had to tell Parker about her stepmother.

Taking her hand when Boss left them, he told her everything that he knew about Angela and the demon Merlin.

"Can he kill her? This demon, can he kill Angela? I don't wish her death either, but I also think that she is going to suffer enough without being brutalized every day." Tholan told her that that Angela had free will. "So, sort of, it's a 'she's made her bed now she has to lie in it' sort of thing?"

"I know that one, and yes, that is what she has to do. She has agreed to have whatever happens to her happen. She might have been tricked in some way, I do not know, but she did make a deal with a demon, and she could not have expected it to be easy on her."

"No. I suppose not." They were in the living room when she smiled at him. "The hot tub, do you understand it now? I mean, I know that we only got to spend a little time in it before Benny called, but you understand now?"

"I do." Tholan grinned. "I should like to see you in it again. That little thing you had on, the bathing suit, it was very pretty on your body. Tell me that you'll wear it for me again sometime soon?"

"I will, big boy. How about right now?"

Tholan felt like his chin hit the floor when she pulled her shirt off her body. Then when her shorts dropped too, he could only stand there and stare.

As Parker walked by him, she closed his mouth and went out the door. Tholan wasn't sure what he was feeling, but it was a feeling that he could get used to. Good heavens, his wife was much more beautiful than he'd thought. And even before, he'd thought her the most beautiful creature of all time.

Following her out to the hot tub, he nearly fell over when she slid into the steaming water and moaned. Tholan felt his cock ache again, his body harden for his wife. And slipping into the water with her, Tholan knew that whatever came next, he was going to be a very happy man.

She came to sit over him, her body lush and wet, dew dripping off the tip of her beautiful nipples. Taking one of the pink tips into his mouth, he nibbled a bit then suckled hard on it. When Parker moaned, he felt his cock stretch even more. It was painfully hard. But after last night's quickie, as Parker had called it, he knew that he'd get relief soon.

"I want to sit on your cock. Ride you." This was new too. He'd been too long at a desk to know all the newest things when it came to sex, but he was willing to try anything with this woman. "Hold your cock, and I'll be able to slide down and over you. That way, I can rock back and forth over you until you want to move again."

"I want to move now." She smiled at him, and when she raised up, he kissed her belly before moving to do as she asked. As soon as she came down over him, slowly — wanting to make him suffer, he knew — Tholan was sure that his head was going to explode with the pleasure of it. "This is riding? I do not believe I have ever seen a horse ridden this way. This is very nice."

As soon as she rolled her hips, her body swaying over his,

Tholan knew that he wasn't going to last long. As she picked up speed, he pulled her breast into his mouth, taking as much as he could into it. When she lifted both of her breasts, pressing them together, he took them both. He needed more, had to have more.

Standing up, her legs wrapped around him, Tholan laid her on the side of the tub. It was all the encouragement that he needed. Tholan took everything that she offered him. He knew, someplace in the back of his mind, that this was too hard on her, but when she cried out that she was coming, he released all his pent-up need into her, pounding her harder to empty himself.

She laid there for several seconds, then rolled to her belly. Standing on the bench in the tub, she told him — nay, ordered him — to take her again. Tholan didn't understand at first, but she cleared that up for him.

Never would he have thought that he could please her so soon; his body was spent. But as soon as she spread her legs for him, Tholan entered her with his hardening cock and nearly fell back when she came right away.

Leaning over her, taking her again and again, he reached down over her belly into her womanhood and pinched the small nubbin that seemed to call to him. As soon as she came again, Tholan bit down on her shoulder as he released again.

Neither of them moved. He was sure that someday in the near future someone would come looking for them and find them just the way they were. Sliding down to sit on the bench again, he held Parker while she slept. This, he knew, would be a memory that he'd never forget.

Taking her up to bed, he lay beside her. He didn't sleep — none of the protectors did — but he did watch her resting. Tholan hadn't thought that he could have been more in love with Parker, but he knew in that moment that he loved her more every day. And he was sure that he would love her more tomorrow. Holding her hand in his, Tholan spent the night just watching and loving her.

Chapter 8

Butch Groves liked that he was a wanted man. It made him feel superior to all the men that he'd shared a cell with back in the day. The FBI was on the lookout for him. His picture was plastered all over the place. Hell, he'd even seen it on the front page of the paper when he'd done a smash and grab just now. Hanna handed him the things that she'd been able to get out of the jewelry store that they'd just robbed.

"We keep this up and we'll be on easy street before we know it." He was kinda hoping that she'd given up on that idea of hers to leave the country. "I'd like a little house with a garden in the back. I don't know what I'd grow—shit, I don't even know how to cook—but it'd look pretty."

"What about Heather? We leave, and she might tell on us. She's got herself a lot of shit on us. And I don't believe for a minute that because she's our kid that she won't have plenty to say." Hanna agreed with him. "I've been all over this town twice and there isn't any sign of her. Not even in the old haunts that she used to run to. I'm just betting that she's stole away on one of them big buses and left us high and dry."

119

"We're better off without her anyway, to my way of thinking. She was getting to be a real stick in the mud about everything. How the hell did she think we kept her fed? Well, fed when we remembered. And some kind of roof over her head?" Hanna snorted. "We sure didn't do it by having a job. Christ, to have her saying that we were bad people, that sure did hurt more than I thought it would."

"We are bad people, Hanna." They both laughed about that. Hanna had been at this game longer than he'd been. Together they had perfected it. Smash and grabs were a big payoff but going into the houses and getting the bigger things, now that was a real joy to be had. "I'll make me one more pass through the town, and if I don't find her, then we'll move on. Like you said, we really don't need her anyway. And if she tells on us, then we'll be out of reach of the cops by then."

"You think my idea is good?" He nodded at Hanna and smiled. "Oh, Butch, you've made me so happy. And without the kid, we'll have so much more room in the house. Not a big one. I just want one that I can roam around in and have a nice day in. Nothing like that one we saw from the woods yesterday. Christ, that house looked like a president or something lived there. I wonder what sort of things they might have in there."

"Maybe we should do that one." She looked at him with a frown. "One for the road. You know that a house that big, it'll have big screen television out the ass. And all kinds of nick-knacks all over the place. Hell, one room alone would buy you a house as big as you wanted, I'm betting."

He could tell that she wanted to do it. The house, even from where they had been, seemed to glow with the need to be robbed. And the cars in the driveway, they looked as prime as anything he'd ever dreamed of having.

By the time they were ready to roll up in their sleeping bags — the tent they'd taken had been a bust — Hanna was on board with him about taking a look at the house. She made him promise that as soon as they were finished they'd be hitting the road.

"Yeah, I promise. Maybe we'll take the pair of cars they had out front." He'd noticed that they were gone when he went to peek on them after supper, but that didn't bother him. They probably put them in that big old garage that was near the house. They were old as hell, and he'd bet even if they didn't drive them to their next place, they'd fetch a nice pretty penny by selling them off. Setting down on the roll he was on, Butch thought again about how he was a wanted man.

When he'd met up with Hanna, she'd just been released from prison. He'd never been in yet, having not really walked the straight and narrow, but having kept his stealing and shit down to where he'd not get a prison sentence with what he took.

Almost as soon as they hooked up, three days after her release, they were hitting the banks around town and a few houses too. Then she got in the family way and he'd had to venture out on his own, just to make ends meet, so to speak. But she was only down for a little while, his Hanna was. As soon as she popped out the kid, she was up and hitting the banks right along with him again.

Heather had slowed them down a bit. They'd have to make sure that they only did their hits when she was asleep. And it seemed to him that she knew when they were ready to go on a job. The kid would scream her head off, and one of them, usually Hanna, would have to stay behind and tend to her. Christ, he'd wished even back then that they'd rid themselves of her rather than carry her around all the damned time.

Nobody knew about Heather. When her time had come, Butch had braved delivering his daughter all on his own. It had been nasty work, and whenever he thought about it, he'd get a little ill to his belly. But he'd done it and regretted not dropping her a few times on her head just so they could be a couple again.

When Heather had turned five, they realized what an asset she'd become. Cute as a button, they'd been told, she'd open the doors to anything that she wanted. Butch decided to have her open a few doors for them, but that had only worked the one time. Then she'd go screaming her fool head off when they told her to do it again. Got some doors open, it did, but also the police called.

Butch loved the sound that the hammer made when it hit a head. He'd been using an axe out in the woods to practice hitting someone hard enough to break through their noodle on the first try. The first time he'd done it, it had nearly taken him to his knees, the need to come had been so strong. After that, it was all he could do not to hit people when they were just walking down the sidewalk.

"Hey, Butch?" He looked at Hanna, thinking that she was asleep. "You think that after we take care of the people in that house, we can live there for a couple of days? Just to see how the other part of the world lives. If you don't wanna, I understand, but it would please me something wonderful to have that for a time."

"You know that I can't deny you anything." He kissed her then and laid back down. "We'll have to make sure that we do this right the first time then. I mean, it'd be best if we caught them outside so that we won't mess up your pretty floors."

"I think I can lure them out. It'll be just like old times for us." He laughed a little, then waited for an hour before he got up and went to the edge of the property to see the house again. He needed to make sure that there wasn't anything roaming the property that would trip them up. Also, any kind of guards around.

It wasn't all lit up like a lot of the houses around this neighborhood. They were all mansions, and he would love to be able to hit them all. Maybe if Hanna liked the place well enough, they could do that before taking off. He looked around the woods then for any sign of someone smoking or having themselves a little get to. A little pot smoking party or something.

People squatted on land all the time. Most of the time they'd just pitch a tent and stay a night or two. If they had a creek or something on the land, they'd get themselves a bath or some fish before taking to the road again. He and Hanna had been there for nearly a week now, and he thought it funny that they'd not seen a single person, not a deer or any other creature, since they'd been here. He knew that they were around. They'd rustle in the woods around them when they were in bed, and the places that they'd pass by would be full of deer shit. Even a couple of times they'd seen the remnants of something's dinner. But never the animal that had done it.

Making his way back to his bag, he thought of Heather. The kid had been getting pretty, but when she was cleaned up, like she liked to be, Heather was really pretty. He knew that people would pay good money for a kid like they had. He didn't want to think about what they'd do to her, but so long as the money was good, Butch didn't care. So long as they didn't try to get a refund when they were finished with her.

Just as he was going to zipper himself in, he saw something

move just beyond their fire. It was low enough that no one from the house could see it, so he wondered if it was one of the other squatters on the land coming to borrow a cup of sugar.

The woman came out of nowhere and smiled at him. "No, I don't need any sugar. I had several tons delivered today, but thanks. I want to know why you're still hanging around here. You have to have something better to do with your time than dirty up the land."

Butch was still trying to wrap his mind around the sugar comment when a man appeared beside her. They were huge, the two of them, and dressed in the cleanest clothes he'd ever seen. When he took a step toward them, just to see if they were real, they sprouted wings, like a fucking bug.

"Why is it that when someone sees us, the first thing they think of is bugs?" The man looked at him. "We're not bugs. We're protectors."

"Protectors, huh? You here to protect me and my wife? I'll have to tell you, I think we've been doing an all right job of that all on our own." The man shook his head and didn't speak again. Butch was sort of uncomfortable with them being there, and decided he'd had enough. "You two, you get on out of here. We've no business with you. And make sure that when you leave, you don't come back either. I've got me some weapons here that will make you so you regret it for a long time."

"We're here to warn you." Butch asked the woman about what. "Your thoughts on Heather. She's in a good place now, and we're warning you to stay way. Or we'll have to do something— Damn it, Valyn, why can't I just kill them both, and we'd not have to worry about it? You saw what he was going to do—sell that little girl to someone that was going to kill her. Not that it's going to happen, but we might be able to save some other kid from their clutches. Let me just hurt them badly enough that they lay out here and bleed to death. I'd feel better. And I know you would."

"Hey." They both turned to him. "What the hell are you talking about, my thoughts? You been listening in on my conversations with my wife? That's not right. And what do you know about Heather? You got her tied up someplace? If you do, then I'm calling the cops."

"Go ahead and do that. Please do that." The woman was being really strange, and Butch found himself looking at the man. "I'll even let you use my phone. Hell, I'll even dial it for you."

"You and her, you married?" The man laughed and said that she was his sister. "Sister, huh? Well, she's a might touched in the head if you ask me. I want you two to get out of here now. I want to get some sleep."

"So you can try and rob the house out there? Won't do you any good to try. There is enough magic around the place that anyone that has ill-will in their hearts won't be able to cross the magic. Also—and this is really important that you know and understand—the man and woman that live there, they won't be as nice as we have been. Especially if you try and take Heather." The man looked at the woman. "Well, as nice as I have been. Judith here, she'd just as soon rid the world of people like you. But I had to explain to her that would make for a very small world. There are a great many bad people like you two out in this realm."

"They got my daughter? That isn't right. What right do they have in taking her? Or are they using her up? That's going to cost them a good bit of money." The man moved so fast that Butch didn't see him. Then something was holding him up in the air and cutting off his wind. Clutching at his throat, Butch knew for sure that he was as good as dead. And he didn't even know what he'd done.

"Valyn, let him go. Valyn. Let him go." The man didn't look like he was going to do it; his face was hard, like it had been set in stone. The woman turned him, shaking him hard, and Butch dropped to the ground. He was trying his best to catch his breath, his head hurt, and his throat felt like he'd been strangled.

Butch looked at the two people and decided that he'd had enough of them. Picking up his axe, he stood up and staggered slightly. As soon as he caught his breath, he was going to deal with them pronto.

Pulling the axe up and over his head, he felt someone behind him. Without even thinking about it, showing these people that he meant business, Butch turned and swung at the same time. He wasn't able to catch himself when he saw who was right behind him. Hanna caught the axe right in her head and nearly all the way to her chest.

She stood there for several seconds, just looking at him with one busted eye and the other cockeyed. When her warm blood hit him in the face, Butch puked. Then she dropped, right on top of him, and the axe hit him in the chest.

~*~

"I'm calling the police and an ambulance. Hang on." Valyn had wanted the man to suffer, but not like this. He was sorry now for what he'd done. "Don't die on me, Mr. Groves. Help is on the way."

Blood spurted from his mouth when he tried to talk. Valyn thought he was asking for the axe to be removed, but he couldn't do that either. He had to keep the crime scene just as it was. But he had a feeling that it was too late for him,

126

and for Hanna, his wife. When he tried to move his arms — to hold his wife, Valyn supposed — all that happened was that he coughed up more blood. He was a goner for sure, Valyn thought.

The sirens were getting closer to them. It was too late for them to do anything for Hanna. The axe had hit her brain and severed her spine. She'd been dead before the axe came to a halt in her chest.

It was the most wonderful sound that he could have hoped for, other than Jenny telling him that she loved him — Boss and Hell showed up just as the man was taking his last breaths. There was no hope for him going with Boss, but both men had to be there when the person hadn't been the best of people. These two, as far as Valyn was concerned, weren't the best of anything other than being bad people.

Boss, the bigger of the two, was dressed all in white. His wings were as snowy looking as a new pillow that hadn't been slept on. Valyn laughed at his own joke but sobered up quickly when Hell looked at him.

Hell, what he'd been called all Valyn's life, was tall but no less big, he supposed. He was dressed all in red, the wings on him as dark as the night, but he could see them well enough. And so could the dead, or in this case dying. Boss spoke to Hell as if they'd been at a picnic and they were having a glass of tea.

"I have his child. She is in good hands. But I should like to have a conversation with you soon. It's about one of your own." Hell rolled his eyes and asked who it was now. "I cannot say his name, you know that. Not here."

"Hey." They turned to look at Butch, who had drawn his last breath and was now among the dead. "What the fuck are you two talking about? Where am I? Where is my Hanna?"

The waiting room was devoid of anything. The walls and the floor were as white as the wings that Boss had. Hell told him, after helping Butch to stand, where he was and where Hanna was.

"So, as you can see, you two are going to live a long time now as workers for me." Butch looked around, and for some reason Valyn thought he was looking for an angle. Something he could use to get out of this. "You can't bargain with me, Butch. It's much too late for that."

"It's never too late to make a deal." Valyn watched as the color, every drop of it, was bled out of Butch. Not just his body, but his clothing as well. Before he left here, like had been done to his wife before him, he'd be dressed all in black and would have a mark on his neck that called him a murderer. "How about you let me and my wife go, and we'll not bother you again. Are you guys the owners of the house out there? If you are, then we can do some business. I won't be robbing you."

Hell looked at Valyn, then at Butch. "You won't be robbing anyone ever again, I'm afraid. You're going to be much too busy for that to happen." Butch asked him what he was going to be doing. "Do you have any idea who I am? Why I'm here?"

"No. I don't care much either, if you want to know the truth. And don't forget, I asked you where my wife was." Hell told him that she was dead and already busy at work. "Work? Hanna has never worked a day in her life. Where is she really?"

With a snap of Hell's fingers, Butch was gone. Hell thanked them both and told Boss that he could see him in the afternoon. When he too disappeared, Boss turned to him, looking as he always did, in jeans and a shirt that had some silly saying on it.

"You did well, son." Valyn told him that he'd wanted to kill the man. "But you did not. And because of your actions, inadvertently, they're off the streets and where they belong."

"I didn't cause their deaths, sir." Boss shook his head and told him that he'd done more than that — he'd tried his best to save him. "He was going to die anyway. I just — I was more concerned with keeping the crime scene clean of Judith and I."

"And for that, I'm grateful too." They were standing in the field that the two bodies were still lying next to. "They will find all manner of things that these two have taken from the homes they've robbed. The axe alone, with the nick in the blade, will be just what the police need to convict them on several deaths as well. Also, you should know that there are no records of Heather's birth. It was a home — well, van delivery, and they never bothered with the paperwork. They were never married legally either."

"They were going to sell Heather to someone that would do to her what was done to Sally. They would have used her up then killed her, wouldn't they?" Boss nodded, and Valyn turned to look at the couple that were being separated by a team of medics. "I feel redeemed."

"You were never responsible for Sally's death, Valyn. I've told you that before. Had you not been there with her, then she would have never been found. Because of your help, the man responsible for so many was caught and hanged. You did a great many children a lot of good by doing just what you were supposed to do."

Valyn felt better than he had in a while. "I'm rested and happy. I have a good wife, a baby on the way, and I have friends. People that I can count on to keep me in line." He thought of Judith and what she'd done to keep him from killing Butch. He told Boss what had happened, as if he didn't already know. "Then he picked up the axe and tried to kill us. We did try our best to get him to move on. To go away and forget this place."

"Even though he would have left, he would have returned. Knowing that his child had it better than them, it would have been too much for them to bear. Now Heather is free to be the child she was meant to be. She has uncles and aunts that will be just as protective of her as her new parents. I cannot thank you enough, Valyn, for doing this for me. I love you, son."

"And I love you."

They turned away when the couple was pulled apart. Hanna's head came off, and one of the medic's puked on Butch. There would still be enough evidence to convict them both. Enough even to give the dead peace. Valyn left for his home—Jenny was there waiting for him.

"Are they taken care of?" He nodded, holding her in his arms as he did every day. The feelings that came over him when he did made him rest easier, his body relax more. "Good. I heard that Parker is taking her to the mall tomorrow. The rest of us are going to show up in time for lunch. We certainly do eat a great deal in this family, don't you think?"

"It's all right. It's good food." She kissed him on the cheek and he picked her up in his arms as he made his way to the living room. "I feel better than I have in a long while. When they were both dying, all I could think about was that I'd done this—that I'd killed them. But then when Boss showed up, I had a feeling wash over me like I'd had a load taken from me and my heart. I told him that I feel like I've been able to vindicate Sally with my actions tonight."

"Good. I'm so glad to hear that." He held her, thinking of

the things he needed to tell the others, the things that Judith had gotten from the surrounding properties. "Judith stopped by. She told me that tomorrow we're going to be taking care of the demon. I hope that Tholan and Parker are ready for this. They're such a cute couple. And so quiet. I also know that she's been working on a few things with the rest of the attorneys that we've hired to get things rolling on the charity fundraisers. I don't understand why we can't just keep it in house."

"The community needs to be a part of this. For no other reason then they'll feel like they're a part of it and won't be shy when it comes time for them to need something from the good works that we're doing. Last week, Mr. Bush came to me about his neighbor, telling me that he thought they'd had their power shut off. It was nothing for me to go down and have it paid for them, but while I was there, I noticed that he, too, was behind in his payments, and was set to be shut off in a few days. He wouldn't have told me about it had he not helped with the fundraisers that we had two weeks ago."

She nodded and snuggled up under his chin. "You're such a good man. As are the rest of the people here. I'm just lucky enough to have ended up with the best of them. You're my hero, Valyn."

He'd never been anyone's hero before. Valyn didn't even think that he'd ever been loved like Jenny did him. As he carried her up to their bedroom, her sound asleep in his arms, Valyn gave thanks, as he did every day, that he had found her—or better yet, that she'd put up with him. Valyn was a very lucky man.

Chapter 9

Hell had no time for this today, but he knew that if the king from the other realm said that he needed to speak to him, then it was important. Last evening was the first time he'd worked directly with him in a long while. As he made his way to the deli, a place that he'd come to enjoy even when he wasn't here on business, Hell ordered a coffee and a blueberry muffin just as Tholan and his mate showed up.

They had mated. It was written as clearly on Tholan's face as it was the young woman's. As happy as he could be for any couple, he was for them. Both had gone through a great deal and had come out on the other end good people.

The child was a surprise. It looked to him as if she had gone through a great deal too. Only in a different way. Abuse, no matter what the kind it was, could make a person into something they normally would not be. The child was terrified of everyone, even the couple, but she was being brave. It took him a moment to realize that it was the child of the couple that he'd taken. Heather, he knew her name to be then and when she went off with one of the others, he sat down.

When the woman—he believed her name to be Parker—sat down across from him, Hell smiled at her. She was a beauty, even in her apparent anger. When she took his muffin he stared at her, thinking that he might not be hurt too much if he didn't laugh at her right now.

"I know who you are. You touch one hair on her head and I will do something really terrible and come to your home town and make you regret it for the rest of your days. Which I will point out won't be all that long if I have to come down there." He said nothing, just watched the fire behind her eyes. "She is nothing like her parents."

"I should hope that she is. Aren't you and Tholan her parents? As far as I know, sickening as I find it, you two are the best that has ever come to this realm." She was shocked, and he loved it. Taking back his muffin, he asked her why he was here.

Like the one they called Boss knew nothing of Hell's realm, he knew nothing of this one. There were things that he could gleam from others around, but nothing solid, nothing concrete. But the woman in front of him, just her anger made him think that she should handle the one that had fucked up so badly that he'd had to be called. She'd make short work of the demon and never bat an eye.

"I have a part of one of your men. A hand, I suppose, that looks like a stick now that it's no longer attached to him." Hell spit out his muffin; it had lodged someplace between his teeth and his neck. Coughing hard, he felt a firm hand on his back, pounding him hard, trying to either break a rib of this form or to dislodge the muffin. "I see that you didn't know that."

"No, I didn't." Taking a drink of the water that was offered, Hell looked at her. "And how is it that you have a piece of him? I'm assuming that you not only know what it

134

means, but his name as well."

"I do. But I have something that I want to ask you first. Not a favor, not really, but something that I'd like to, I guess, bargain with." He nodded for her to go on. "There are two of your...men, I guess...tormenting me. And, yes, I have both their names. But the one that I'm going to give you is the one I want to bargain with. He's claimed my stepmother. Not that I give a shit what happens to her—she was instrumental in me not getting to spend the final days with my da when he died—but I don't want her to suffer as she is, not by this demon's hand."

"You said that there are two of them that you're dealing with. I see. I had no idea that you were even having trouble with one of them." He refilled his cup of coffee and had a glass of juice set in front of Parker. "These two demons, do they know of each other?"

"Yes, the one I have a piece of, he did something to Angela that sort of sold her to this other demon. While, as I said, I could care less, I don't want her to suffer by anyone else's hand but my own." He laughed. "You wouldn't think this was so funny if you knew my plans for her."

"I could look, I suppose. Not for the names—I cannot do that—but your plans for your stepmother. What has this first demon, the one that sold her, done to you?" She told him what Angela had done. "I'm sorry, but that's not possible. If she is only...unless he doesn't know that you're only her stepdaughter. I'm guessing that is it. Not that you'd know yet, but the only way that he could have you is if your biological mother sold you to him."

"I didn't know, as you have guessed." Boss sat beside her, and he too had a muffin, but his looked to be berry. He loved all manner of sweets, but muffins, the way they were made

135

here, were his all-time favorite. "I was just telling him what my bargain is."

"I want you to know that while I didn't put her up to this, I do applaud her for what she's doing." Hell had a feeling that Boss might not know her plans for her stepmother. Or he did, and it wasn't nearly as bad as the woman thought. "The couple, they are faring well with you?"

"They are busy." And they were too. Hell had assigned the two of them to clean up the cinders that were shat out of his ass and take them to the incinerator. He didn't really need them to do that, but it was fun hearing them complain. It was what he lived for most days. "About this bargain. What happens to your stepmother after I step in? There are times when it might be too late for you to save her."

"I don't want her saved. I don't think she'd even welcome me stepping in this far. And I'm not doing this for her, but for my da. I think at one time he might have loved her, and that is the only reason I'm doing this." Hell nodded. He liked this woman more and more with each minute. "If you would do this for me, make me a promise only that the demon that hurts her is taken care of, then I will tell you his name."

"And the other? What will happen to him?" She said that she was going to deal with him, but he could be there. "Well, thank you so very much. What, may I ask, is your plan?"

"You cannot. Trust me when I tell you that when I am finished with him, you won't have enough of him left to punish. If you do that sort of thing to demons like him." He said nothing. Hell was sure that she'd not be able to take in what he did to those that he punished. He had only to show her Markum to let her see that he was not a man to trifle with. "Do we have a deal?"

"Yes." He put out his hand and she just looked at him.

136

"Unlike those that work for me, you can take my hand as freely as you would your king's. I do not need to lie and cheat to get what I want. Most of the time, it is offered up to me without any kind of fight."

She took his hand and the power of her pure white magic burned him. Not only was this woman as good as any he'd ever come across before, but she might well be up there with her own king. Hell looked at Boss and noticed his smile. He had a feeling that this man had plans for this couple that went well beyond training the others in how to do their job.

"His name is Merlin. Do your guys get to pick their names? If so, you need a book for them to choose from. Merlin was a good wizard. He had some bad traits too, but for the most part, he was a good guy." He didn't say anything to her, but she might be right. It would be easier for them to choose from, too. "You'll make sure that he releases my stepmother, right?"

"Yes, and there will be no stipulations on this. I could just have her released, her body left as it is, but I won't. For you. You must learn to bargain with better demands. I believe that is where most humans fail." She smiled at him, and Hell, for the first time in his entire existence, felt a shiver of fear. "You knew that. You were perhaps counting on me to be honest? Or were you hoping that I would leave her as she was?"

"I'm going to take care of the other demon at six tonight. How will I contact you with the place?" He said that she only had to think of him, that they had a connection. It didn't go unnoticed by him that she had not answered him, but he let it go for now. "I will take care of him. You step in and I will do more to you than him. Understand?"

"I do. But if you fail, you will give me something of yourself." She said no. "Just like that, a no? What if I should strike a bargain with you? Would you be more receptive then?"

"No, I say no because I will not fail. This guy, this thing, has fucked with me enough. He will rue the day that he tried to take me." Again, the shiver of fear. "Do you wish to be there still?"

"Yes, I would like to see you at work." He stood up when she did. "It will be a pleasure to watch you, I think. I will be honest with you, Parker—I can almost feel sorry for the demon that has dared to fuck with you. I honestly do."

"Oh, trust me when I tell you, he will be sorry. As sorry as I can make the fucker."

Hell was laughing as he made his way to the counter. He would pay for his meal, even though Parker had eaten most of it. But when he reached the counter, Judith, another one of the king's children, handed him a large container and told him thanks.

"I must pay you for these." She shook her head and he peeked inside the box. "There are a great many muffins in here. I should not like to be responsible for you going out of business. I have come to enjoy the treats that you make."

"I won't. But you do this for her, let her do this her way, and I'll make sure that you have a box like this weekly. Not that I want you to sway things in her favor—I just want you to stand back and let her do this her way. I think they both, her and Tholan, need this more than anyone knows." He knew that as well. Taking the box, he put a hundred-dollar bill in the tip jar. "Thank you for that. The staff, they're donating everything in that to buy tickets at the next charity event. We're giving away a college education, a full ride to a college of the winner's choice."

Hell moved out of the building and to his own realm.

Snapping his fingers, he put nine more of the large bills in the jar and smiled. It wasn't like him to be an upright person, but he had had a good morning. And he had a box of muffins all of his own. Sitting in his chair, he contemplated the plan. Taking a muffin and eating it, he decided to get the first part of this over with.

Calling to Merlin, he wasn't the least bit surprised when he came to him in human form and naked.

"You have been to the other realm? Without my permission?" There was blood on his body, and he reeked of human. More than likely Hell did as well, but he was in charge, not the minions that worked for him. "You have taken a human form for what reason, Merlin? And to be so covered in blood, you must tell me who it is I have to look for when they arrive."

"I have.... She is.... You would not know her, my lord. She is nothing but a bit of pussy that we enjoy. I mean that we both enjoy. She and I, we enjoy what we are doing together." He told him that he was stuttering. "Yes, I am.... You called me at a bad time. I was close."

"Close? Then I shall return you." He was gone in that moment, and Hell followed him. "You are telling me that she enjoyed this from you?"

The room was destroyed. There was blood, hers, all over the room, and parts of her as well. Hell picked up a finger and showed it to Merlin. He only smiled and took it from him. Then he looked at the woman.

She would not survive. Even with the immortality that had been given to her, the way it was worded would not allow her to live through this. He could save her, but she would never be the same. Her head was nearly gone; her fingers had been bitten off and spit around the room so that they looked like a nightmarish sort of artwork lying on the table by the couch. Nine of them looking like petals of a bloodied flower.

Her thighs were burnt to the bone, and even those were dry and brittle. He wondered what Parker would say when she saw the mess that she'd become. Looking at Merlin, he told him to finish.

"Finish? I cannot, my lord. You are here." He crossed his arms over his chest, not saying a word but waiting for him to do as he'd bidden. "Sir, she is mine. I have taken her as my own."

"Then you will not mind that I watch the two of you at play. Though, I have to tell you, Merlin, she does not look to me as if she is much of a participant. Are you using your magic to keep her alive for you to make suffer?" He had his answer, and it pissed him off. "You have. You have broken not only our laws by doing this, but you have made a human suffer unnecessarily. What do you have to say for yourself? And I do not expect you to give me half-truths, Merlin. I want to know what you were doing here with this nearly dead human."

He could tell that he was apprehensive of performing in front of him. He also knew that, while the man boasted that he had a big cock, he had nothing more than a nubbin, and even that would not satisfy the most horny of women. Hell told him once more that he was to do it or he would, and the man backed up, just as Hell had thought he would.

"All right then, bend over." Shock was written as plainly on his face as it might have been on anyone's. "I said that I would finish, and you are in such obvious pain from not coming."

Hell bent at the waist, looking hard for the cock that the man was saying was ready. He asked him if he was ready still

140

as he could not tell, when Merlin, in all his stupidity, drew back and hit him.

~*~

Tholan looked at the body that had once been a woman. He had told Parker that he would come here when the police had called her. Benny asked him if he was all right when he turned his back to what was left of Angela Brooks.

"He made her suffer in ways that I am not sure that anyone could have guessed." Benny nodded and said that she'd been barely alive when he'd arrived. "Do not tell Parker that. She has been crying since the call came in. If not for Heather, I think she might have gone to her bed for the day. But they are shopping and getting ready for school."

"I won't tell her. But if you can tell me that it's Angela, I can have her body removed. Lily came by; everyone here sees that she died from a drug overdose. I don't think even my seasoned men could have handled this." Tholan told him that was a good idea as well. "Hell was here too when I arrived. He had a message for me to give to Parker. Will you pass it on?"

"I will." Tholan nodded when he'd been told. "I think that he is in awe of her. She bravely stood up to him several times today at the deli."

"I heard. I guess she also stole his muffin. Judith said that he's been in several times to get a few of them. Usually he never stays, but today, when he did, she said that she boxed him up some to take." Tholan glanced at the body again. "What will happen now?"

"She is to be cremated, from what I was told about her arrangements. And once she is, then she will be buried next to Parker's father. It is only fitting, she told me." Benny told him that wasn't what he'd meant, but that was good of her. "I know that. I just did not want to think about what she is going to be doing today. She plans to beat the devil at his own game, or in this case, a demon. Do you think that they will leave us alone after this? She plans to make them think that they will all get this should they come sniffling around."

"Sniffing. But I don't know. I wasn't born to this group—I only married into the magic. But I have noticed, as everyone has, that she is stronger than anyone that I've met. I won't say this in front of Lily, but even stronger than her."

They both laughed, and when the body was gone, some of the protectors from the compound came in to ask if they could take care of the room.

Tholan knew that Boss had sent them. The room would never be the same if he hadn't. There would be no trace of the carnage that had gone on in this room. The soot on the walls, the blood in the carpet. The furniture, all of it, would be destroyed—they were only splinters of wood and material anyway.

Benny gave them his permission and the room was cleared of everything but the walls. In moments, less he thought, the room would look as pristine as it had when it had been new. Angela's home, too, would go to Parker, and she said that she'd turn it over to one of the charities so that they could use it for a home for someone that was in need. Parker would also fill the rooms with the needed furniture.

When he was finished at the little house, he met Parker and Heather at the mall. There were already several bags of things, he noticed, as well as a stack of books. Picking up one of them, his heart melted when Heather looked up at him and asked if he'd read it to her.

"I will. I love this story. You will too, I think. It's about a family that is living on an island after their ship was

142

destroyed." He noticed that she had several of the classics, as well as some mysteries and fantasies. "You are trying to find what you like?"

"Parker told me that reading several kinds, it'll help me learn faster and figure out what I enjoy the most. I've never had a book of my own before. The library, they wouldn't let me check them out anymore because Dad would ruin them." She touched the covers of the stack. "They smell good too, don't they? Parker said you like to read too."

Embarrassed to be found out, he told her that he did love to read. Tholan liked romance books. The more romance, the better as far as he was concerned. While he didn't have a favorite author, he picked his books out by their covers. He had seen once where as much time was spent choosing a cover as was spent writing the books.

"It's something that I do when everyone else is asleep." He watched her with the books. They seemed to mean more to her than even the clothes and shoes. "Did Parker tell you that you're going to visit Riss and his wife again? Not for all night, but for a visit. I think that they're ordering pizza again."

"No, they said burgers."

When he saw the other women, he stood up. Neither of them talked about Angela other than for Parker to ask him if it was done. When everyone was seated, there were decisions about where to eat, and then they all left for the different places.

Heather stayed with him. "Parker told me that my mom and dad are dead. That they killed each other by accident. Was it drugs?"

"No, not drugs." He and Parker had decided that if she wanted the truth, they'd give it to her, but for now, a watered-down version. "Do you want to know how, or would you like for me to tell you that I saw them, and they are very much gone?"

"That way." He nodded, and when she stood up, he thought she was going to join the others, but she crawled up into his lap. "I like not being all doped up any more. I can think. Can you think when you're drugged up?"

"I don't use drugs—I never have. Not even for a headache." He'd never had one of those either but didn't mention that. "Are you happy living with us, Heather?"

"Yes. Very much. I like having a bed and a shower that I can use anytime I want. Yesterday I took three of them. Parker told me that she thought that I'd not want to do that after a while. I don't know. I really like being clean. And I can use a brush in my hair. I got my own brush and some pretty ties too. I'm going to have ponytails when we get home."

"Good for you. I love ponytails on little girls." She was quiet for a time, and he watched Parker as she spoke to Jenny. They were in the line for Chinese food. Tholan had to smile when the woman behind the counter greeted them in her language.

"I was wondering something. When you get more kids, will you put me out to pasture?" He asked Heather why she'd think that. "I don't know. That's what my dad used to say to my mom when she asked him if she was looking her age. I don't know what that means, but if you do it, can I go there with a shower?"

"Absolutely. If we put you out to pasture, you will most assuredly have a shower. I think that's all the fashion now. To have a shower in a pasture." She giggled, and he tickled her. "We won't do that even if we have a hundred other children. You are and always will be our little girl, even when you're old like me."

144

"You're not old." Tholan laughed again. If she only knew. "When you go and see the demon tonight, are you going to kill him?"

Before he could ask her where she'd heard about that, Kala told him not to lie. She was looking at them, and that made the link they were talking through seem all the louder for her caution. *Don't lie to her, thinking that she's not old enough to know. She is older than the dirt for all that she's endured for one so young.*

"I'm not going to fight him, Parker is. She will win, if you're worried about that." Heather said that she wasn't. "To be honest with you, I'm a little nervous about it, but I know the rules better than most for our kind, and I think she'll come out a winner."

"I do too. When that lady at the store told me that I was a size too small for my age, Parker got all up in her grill. I never seen anybody fight for me before. She can sure be scary, huh?" Tholan said that she could be and asked about the lady. "She assumed—that's what Parker said she was doing—that I was only six. I said I was nine and the lady just tsked at me, like I was lying. Before I could put the dress back that I wanted to try on, she took it from me and handed me a littler one. I saw Parker coming toward me and I backed up. I could see her meanness a mile away."

"Was she mean or defending you?" Heather looked at him. "There is a difference. Mean means that she was just being rude to the woman for no reason. Defending you means that she was making sure that you were treated as you should have been, and not the way the woman was doing to you."

"Defending, then, but I still moved out of the way." Heather snuggled under his chin and he held her. "Can I call you Dad?"

It took him several seconds to realize what she'd said to him. Or for his heart and mind to be on the same page with each other. He needed to do this right. To say the wrong thing, he knew, would make her hate him.

Just say yes, Tholan. He did so and glared at Kala. *You men take the longest time to get around a bush than anyone I have ever known. When someone asks you if you want to be Dad, you say yes. Or hell yes. See how easy that is?*

I wanted to do this right. Kala told him that he had — he'd said yes. *What if she wanted more than that?*

Then she would have asked you. I'm sure that when she has a question, about anything, she comes to you or Parker, right? He told Kala that she did. *Then you should know that this isn't any different. 'Can I call you Dad?' That should have been a no brainer. Don't go looking for trouble when the answers to the problem are right there.*

Food was brought to them then. They had all gotten something different so that they could share. Heather seemed to be all right now, when they were together like this, and had no trouble voicing her opinion on certain things. Tholan noticed that she liked Chinese as much as he and Parker did.

By the time they were finished shopping, Tholan was sure that they'd walked nine hundred miles, entered every shop at least three times, and had enough junk food, it had been called, to fill a truck. But they were happy, and so was he. The limo pulled up just as they were stepping out of the large building. Tholan thought that he could get used to this sort of service. Now he only had to think about tonight.

Chapter 10

Parker was about asleep when she sat down on the couch. What with last night in the hot tub and today at the mall, she thought that if she slept for a month, she'd still be exhausted. But boy, was she relaxed. Thinking about Tholan and making love to him had her smiling. He sat down at the end of the couch and picked up her feet to massage them.

"Heather has decided to go to Riss's now. The babies are a big draw for her, I think. And I sent her some jammies and slippers. Kala said that way if it was too late or if we needed to rest up, she'd be ready for that too." Parker moaned when he hit the spot on her foot that was hurting the most. "I think that if you were naked, I could massage your back too." He wiggled his brows at her and she laughed.

"I don't need to be naked for you to massage my back. But I do like where your mind is going." He'd shown her last night how she could be dressed and undressed with her magic. Using it now, she watched the hunger in his eyes as he looked down her body. "I can feel your cock under my toes."

She massaged his cock with her foot. And when he turned

147

on the couch so that he was facing her, she sat up and reached for his mouth. The man could kiss like it was his job, and she felt her own hunger spiral out of control.

"When you rode me last night in the water, I could only imagine what it would feel like on a bed or couch. Please, love, ride me now." She sat up over him, his cock so hard now that she could almost come. When he was naked too, she slid down over him and moaned again. "You are so warm over me. I love that I can be a part of you and touch you at the same time."

"I love that too." When he took her breast into his mouth, she pulled him closer. "Nibble on my tips, like you did last night, Tholan."

With every thrust she could feel him surging upward. His hands at her hips would leave a mark, she knew that, but with this newfound power, she'd be healed almost before she realized that they were there.

"I love your breasts. They are so full and soft. And your nipples are long and chewable." He bit down on her right breast and she nearly came again. "Come for me, Parker. I want to feel you tighten around me again. I love the way your sheath squeezes and milks me."

She came hard, holding onto him for fear of flying away. And when she was ready again, Tholan took her to the couch as she wrapped her legs over his hips. Parker could almost feel his cock at the back of her throat. And each time that he filled her, his cock moving in and out of her, Parker could feel another release coming up, the way it ran along her skin, tightened her throat. And when he came, his body rising up over hers so that his cock didn't just fill her but became a part of her, Parker screamed out his name, over and over, until he dropped over her.

He wasn't finished with her, it seemed, when he took them both to the floor. His cock pounded her hard — his body seemed to be trying to become a part of her. And when he grabbed her breast, tugging at it tightly, she came a second, then a third time. When she lay limp on the floor, his body atop hers in a way that had her completely covered, Parker closed her eyes and let sleep, rest, finally take her.

"You will come to me now." Parker looked at the demon and smiled at him. "You will come to me now before the day is out. Something has happened to my friend, and I fear that I am next."

"Oh, and why should I give a shit about you or your friend? In fact, I'd love it if you just fucked the hell off and left me and mine all alone. You're a pain in the ass." He thanked her but told her to hurry. "I'll be there when I get there. You go away, and I'll see you later. You're fucking up my nice buzz."

"Buzz? I don't understand. And you will notice that I don't appear to care either. Come to me now, or I shall come to you." She didn't answer him. This was just what she was hoping for when Merlin disappeared. "Did you not hear me? I said to come to me."

"I heard you, and like I said, I just don't care. Now, if you want to get this over with, then I suggest that you meet me here, in my yard out back, at six o'clock. That way, should you make a mess, I can have the gardeners clean it up and perhaps you'll be fertilizer for the trees." He growled at her and Parker laughed. "You are so predictable. Why would you want to come here and waste my time on a fight that you know as well as I do that you cannot win?"

"I will win, and when I take you to my lair, I will show you how predictable I can be. I can do things with my cock that will astound you." She asked him what he thought predictable meant. "I don't care. I will see you at six, and make sure that you have taken care of all your things too. Your mother, she has it in her heart that living in your big house will be the best thing that could happen to her."

Waking up, Tholan was staring down at her. With a quick kiss to her mouth, she felt his cock move inside of her. This time when he took her, it was hard—wonderfully, painfully so—and she cried out her release five times before he took his own.

"I am so sorry." Parker stretched and asked him why. "I have harmed you. I don't know what came over me, but it was necessary that I take you that way, to mark you with not just my semen, but with all of me. Even my hands and mouth."

"Not all the time, but when you have a desire to take me that way again, you do it. It was wonderful, and very stress relieving." He grinned. "You are getting used to this, aren't you? The two of us being a couple."

Willing them to their bed, she and Tholan spent the next hour just touching and talking. He was building her up, she knew that. Telling her that she was perfect, that she'd win this. Parker hoped so—she needed to. All this, all this going down, was going to solve a great many problems for a lot of people. The promise that she'd gotten from the king of the other world, the one she'd asked for when everyone else was shopping, was going to make it so the protectors, all of them, were protected themselves. She had his word on it.

Making a bargain with the devil seemed like a stupid thing to do, but she trusted him. She had no idea why, but Parker decided that she would, and he told her that she was either very brave or very stupid. Parker thought she was a great deal of both.

And this promise for them to be safe from my underworld, what will happen to my people should they go against what I have put forth? You know as well as anyone, I cannot see beyond my realm any more than your king can see beyond his. She told him that they'd get the same as the demon today. *Ah, this showdown, you're calling it. And you are that sure that you will win? I don't think I've been that sure of anything for a good long time.*

On my father's soul, I will win this today. Because I know something that you do not. I know that my love for him is as pure and as heartful as his was for me. I do this for him. Hell, as he said he liked to be called, told her that was a great deal of love. *I have that much and more for the family that I now have too.*

Your daughter and husband, I take it. She told him it was all protectors and mystics, including Boss. *I see. All right, Parker. You win today, and I will show my people just what it will be like to fuck with you. And I swear to you, I will tell you each time I hear about them breaking this law.*

And I will you as well before I take action. He told her that was more than he could have hoped for. *Thank you. You're not completely evil, are you?*

I am. You have just caught me on a good day.

He was still laughing when the connection closed. After that, Parker devoted all her energy and attention to those around her, especially her daughter. Heather was going to be as loved and as happy as Parker had ever been with her da.

At four o'clock, they got up and showered together. Tholan messed up three jokes that he'd heard, and she still laughed with him. After they dressed, they made their way to the decking that surrounded their home. The rest of the mystics and a few others that she didn't know were already there. Thinking about his last joke, she smiled.

Parker decided that she was going to get Tholan a knock-

151

knock book and let him try those first. She thought that he needed to work up to the kind of jokes where there was a punch line. His delivery was all wrong.

At five minutes until six, Hell showed up. He was dressed as a business man until Judith took him to task. Then he sat on the deck chair, beer in hand, shorts and a dirty T-shirt on. She helped him hide out by putting a shield of magic around him. So long as he didn't move too much, she could make it so no one knew he was there until it was time.

Warrior—or Rollin, she'd found out was his real name—showed up at fifteen after the hour. She'd expected him to be late and didn't say a word to him when he simply appeared in the yard. Making her way out to him, she knew that Tholan was behind her.

"Two for the price of one? How lovely. Why are you giving me such a treat, Parker Jane Brooks?" She told him that she was not. "When two come out onto the field that is for bargains, I will take you both. That is my rule today."

"Fuck your rules. Now, as I was saying earlier, you said that you wanted to get this finished, as you are missing a friend of yours. I know where he is." He didn't look convinced. "He's been destroyed."

"You are so laughing. You cannot destroy a demon any more than I can one of your kind. Don't lie to me again." His voice had gone hard, like he was trying his best to make a point. "Now, I'm here to get my piece, and you are to come with me. I'm sick of waiting around for you to come to me. A deal is a deal."

"There was no deal for that. You want your piece, you have to win it." Rollin stomped his foot, and that made her laugh. "What? Did you need a nap? That's the way small children act when they've missed their nap time. Shall we put this off for another day? So that you might get one in?"

"You will stop this teasing of me this moment." She closed her mouth, but Parker was far from finished with him. "Now, as I was saying, the two of you will come with me as soon as you turn over my piece. It has been most terrible of you to have kept it for this long. How would you like it if I kept something that belonged to you?"

"You did. I'm here about that as well." Rollin looked confused. Parker was pretty sure that it was a way of life for him, to be confused all the time. "You killed, or were directly responsible for the death of, a family member. And today, this night, you'll pay for that as well."

"I have no idea what you're talking about. You hand over the piece you took from me, and then we'll be on our way. I don't know who that is behind you, but that will be my bonus for having to put up with your sniveling mouth for the last weeks." She asked him what he was talking about, her voice as calm as Boss's when he spoke to them. "You forget? You did nothing but cry and beg for me to be nice to you. Or perhaps that was someone else. No matter. I am finished with this game of yours. Hand it over or die."

"What is my full name?"

~*~

Warrior told her. "You are Parker Jane Brooks. Now, you must be tired of this. I know that I am." She told him that he was wrong. "Nay, never on this. I was given your full name by your mother. A reasonable sort, if you ask me."

"I didn't. What is my full name?" Warrior wasn't sure what she was doing, but he told her again. "Nope. Wrong again. If you'd like, we can come back to that one. When you've had more time to think about it. Who is my mother?"

"Are you going to do this all night? I have shit that I want to get done. Tying you to my cell wall. Fucking you until you're nothing but flesh. Those are on my list for every day, and I do not have time for this. Your mother's name is Angela Brooks. She may have a maiden name, but I don't need that. Just her married name."

"Wrong." Warrior was getting sick of that word. He knew that he wasn't wrong. And she was toying with him again. "You have one more try on my name, and two more on my mother's name. Let's see if you can get my birthdate right."

"What do you mean, I have only a few more tries on your name? There is no rule for that. This is not a childhood faerie tale. There will be as many tries as I need to get it right. Even though I have had it right every time." The man behind her cleared his throat. "What is it? You have something to add to this?"

"I do. According the handbook that was written long ago, there are only three tries to each question. Three questions, three tries. If you fail that, you can buy more tries. It will be up to the soul as to what the fee will be." He looked at the man. "I have studied these laws since the day I was created."

Created? Children of this realm were not created. They were born of a female's body like all the species of this place. The only thing created, besides his kind, were—

"You brought a protector to the field? What is wrong with you? I cannot deal with this. Come with me and we will be finished today." Warrior put out his hand, fully expecting her to take it. "Did you not hear me? Come with me now."

"What is my birthdate?" Warrior took a step toward her. He wasn't going to play anymore. But when she reached up her hand, he covered his own and stepped back when a sword appeared in her hand. "What is my birth—?"

"May twenty-third." He rattled off the year too. "This is

correct too. Your mother's name is Angela Brooks. Your name is Parker Jane Brooks. Now, I said to come with me."

The shift from demon to beast wasn't as easy as it had been before she'd gotten a piece of him. He would never show her that. Warrior wouldn't want her to have any knowledge of him. When she laughed, Warrior stomped his foot. Trees trembled in the aftermath, but none of them fell, much to his anger.

"You got that right. Now, you have no more guesses on my name. What is the name of my mother?"

He growled, spewing his hot breath and spittle on the ground. Where he was hoping that it would catch fire, all it did was sputter and go out. Anger surged through him like a hot blade. He lunged at her and felt the blade of her sword cut deeply into his gullet. Screaming out the name of her mother, he fell to the ground. He was going to end this, even if he had to cheat.

"Would you like to buy more guesses?"

~*~

Hell watched the people on the field. He almost wanted her to lose so that he could take her for his own. She was a good fighter; her stance was that of a warrior. Her blade as she held it was nothing like anything that he'd ever seen before.

"I do not wish to buy more guesses. I am correct." She said that he wasn't. "Then you tell me what you have changed it to. So that you are aware, you cannot do that just to mess me up."

Tholan nodded. This was another person that Hell was impressed with. Not only did he know the laws, but he could quote them better than Hell could. And if pressed, Hell knew that Tholan would know the page number as well as which paragraph it was in. When he told Parker that Rollin was

155

right, the moron jumped up and down like a small child.

He was going to suffer. Hell could see that now. Not only was Rollin a moron, but he had yet to figure out that he was going to be destroyed. Not by him, nay, but by the slip of a woman in front of him. When Boss sat beside him, a beer in his hand as well, he bumped his can to his and it changed into a glass of amber liquid for him, and Boss now had a glass of tea.

"She will win this." Hell nodded and drank down his liquor. "You should give her a boon. I have one in mind for her. She is making it so that we do not have to meet up like this again. I think that deserves something."

"You did not know that she asked for a promise from me?" Boss shook his head, but he didn't look all that surprised. "She asked that all protectors and mystics be safe from my kind forever. When I asked her how that was to work, she reminded me that they have been hurt several times over the years. She said that I had only to show them what happens here today, and they will leave them alone."

"You believe her?" Hell nodded. "I do as well. She is terrifying, is she not? I think that in her mightiness, she might be more petrifying than Michael should I need her to be. And Tholan. I have never seen him so relaxed, so ready to come to my aid. Before, he was as timid as a mouse. I feared that he would be eaten alive by his mate. But they are a pair of matched bookends like I have never seen before."

The blade came down on the foot of Rollin. When he screamed in pain, Parker asked him again if he wanted to buy more guesses. This time he told her that he would buy them with money. Parker only laughed.

"You are not doing this fairly, you know that, don't you?" She nodded and said that she was following the rules. "I have given you your name. I have said that of your mother. You are not doing what is right by the rules of the land."

"My name is Parker Jane Daniels." The slice to his belly brought a vomitus-like spilling of hot juices. As it spilled onto the ground, it was eaten up by the earth. Hell knew that it would be in his realm when he returned. He'd made *this* bargain with Boss. "My mother's name was Grace Jane Elliot Brooks."

This slice removed his legs on his left side. It was too late for Rollin to shift. Too much of his body now lay on the ground before him. And when she stabbed at him again, Rollin not only lost his right eye, but a part of his head as well. This too spilled lava, while his eye spewed a green vileness that even Hell thought too nasty. As the sack that his eye was in shrank and shriveled, so did Rollin. He was screaming for fairness, for the reason for the name changes. Even as he lay there, his body boiling in his own juices, he demanded that she come with him.

"Angela Brooks wasn't my mother, you sick fuck—she was my stepmother, and had no rights to bargain with you at all for me." Tholan read the laws regarding blood relations, and when he got to the part where a stepmother could bargain with a demon, there had to be one biological parent alive when the deed was done, but only if the person was yet a child. Parker was well old enough to make her own decisions, and her father had been alive up until she was an adult.

Rollin was nothing but pieces, pieces that could come back to together in time and form him again—however, not without the last piece of him, the one that Parker had. Parker stood over his body, her blade at the ready, and Hell stood up. As he made his way to the field, he peeled off his mask, taking the form of his true self as he watched the final breaths of his demon.

Few had seen him as such. Hell knew just what he looked like—the fiery demon that was portrayed in books. The only difference was, he did not have a pointed tail, he had pointed spikes. His eyes were red in anger, as they should be. His skin, scales and all, was just as hot and poisonous as everyone thought. He was, after all, the king of Hell.

"Master." It was difficult to understand Rollin; his mouth had been split open, His chin no longer attached to his face. His ears, too, were spread out on the lawn, and the tongue that had told so many lies today was half gone—Rollin held it in his hand. "She has harmed me. I would wish that you were to take me with you when you go. I shall need a few days of healing before I can bring her to you."

"This woman that you have said you would tie to your walls? This same one that you promised to Merlin? You now give her to me? I think not, Rollin. I believe that she has done just what she told me she would to you." Rollin shook his head, trying to beg him again for help. "Nay, I shall not help one such as you. Even for a demon, I am ashamed of what you have done. You bargained for the wife of a protector."

"No." Hell nodded and asked Parker if she was finished. With a shake of her head, Rollin screamed again. "Take me with you. I command that you do."

"You command me? I think that you are in the wrong place if you think to command anyone right now. Rollin, you have been beaten. Just give her what she wants and she will finish you. And in case you don't understand, she is going to destroy you for what you have heaped onto her family." Rollin told him that the stepmother had lied to him. "Yes, so she did, and you punished her even before you knew that. To have signed her over to Merlin, without my permission, is something that I would like to have taken you to task for."

"Take me. Take me and punish me. I wish for it." Hell shook his head. "I beg of you to take me away so that I can be a better demon, my lord. Please. She will destroy me should you not."

"She is going to destroy you anyway. I came here to watch her do it." Hell looked at Parker, then at Tholan, before addressing Rollin again. "And to think I doubted that she could do it. Do you have any idea what kind of protector can do this? What sort of woman it would take to kill a demon such as yourself? One of the most powerful beings that I have ever had the pleasure of meeting. That's right, pleasure. You have made your bed, Rollin; now you must lie in it."

Hell looked at Parker again. Telling her to finish it, he was glad more than he could put to words that he wasn't near her when she brought the blade down a final time. It not only removed Rollin's head, but it split him in two. His body not only shriveled up, but it incinerated in seconds, much like he'd been put into the pits of Hell's home, as it should have been.

When he was gone, his body no more, Parker handed Hell the last piece along with a pair of oddly colored socks.

Rollin the Warrior—Warrior to those who'd had the misfortune of knowing him—was no more.

Chapter 11

Tholan let her sleep. Today was going to be a big day for Parker, and he wanted her to have as much rest as she could get. Not that he feared things would not go her way—he knew that they would—but she had been up and down all night, sick to her belly.

When he made his way down the stairs, Heather was waiting on him. Today was a big day for her as well. She was going to have her first day of school. She, too, had been up all night, but not sick to her belly. Heather wanted to have the perfect outfit to wear so that she'd be just like everyone else.

"Are you ready? Kipling said that he'd come by to get you today so that you'd not have to ride the bus." Heather asked if she looked all right. "I think you the prettiest little girl in the whole wide world, and I would know. I have been around for a long time."

They had finally told her what they were. She had taken it like she did most things—lots of questions and a great many touches. Tholan had learned that there were people who learned by teaching, while others learned by touching.

161

Heather was like the latter of the two. And he had enjoyed watching her face when he'd given in and flown the skies with her.

"I have everything on my list. And I brought me a sweater in case the room is cold. Kip told me that wolves like the rooms cooler because they burn more energy." Tholan told her that was correct. "Dad, do you think Mom will be all right? She looked sort of green the other morning."

"I'm sure that it's just nerves. And if she's still sick after today, she promised me that she would go to the doctor." He looked up the stairs when he heard the door open. They both waited to see if Parker would join them, but she didn't. Another trip to the bathroom, he supposed.

They had their breakfast, each of them having eggs and bacon. It wasn't his favorite meal this time of day—he had grown very fond of the colorful flakes that came in a box, but he was trying to make a good example. After Heather left, he'd have some cereal.

Kipling would take her to the pack school, then make his way to his own classes. The kid was getting bigger every time he saw him. Someday, he decided, if one came their way, he would like to raise a little boy into manhood. He thought it would be fun. Heather certainly was.

He loved the new kitchen. While he wasn't positive what all the new pieces did, he particularly loved the new fridge. The way all he had to do was push a few of the little buttons and it told him what was inside. Also, and the part he loved the most, they could leave notes for each other. The rest of the house was finished now, and he made his way to the living room to read the paper. This room, too, was nice to be in.

Waking Parker up at noon—they had to be at the courthouse at two—he was glad to see she was feeling a little better. Dressing in something comfortable, they made their way to her new car. He had yet to learn to drive, but he would never ride with Dusty again. She had a meanness in her that made his belly ill when they got to wherever they were headed. Heather couldn't ride with her either. Parker thought that it was a hoot riding that fast.

There were so many people standing outside the courthouse, Tholan thought that the hearing had been canceled. But when he got to the door, people allowing the two of them to go through, he could see that there was no room for anyone else in the seats. People were even standing around the outside edges of the seats, there were so many people about.

When they were brought to order, several people stood up and told the judge, Judge Brown, that they thought Parker had gotten a bum deal. Parker explained that to him. He was getting better at sayings, but sometimes he was still tripped up, as Heather told him.

Everyone settled down when Judge Brown told them that he'd like to see that for himself. There were several people in the room that had been at her first trial. The only people absent, ones that Parker wanted there, were Angela, so she could tell them what her part in all this had been, and her da.

"Mrs. Daniels was convicted on all counts, Your Honor. I haven't any idea why she thinks that this is going to solve anything." The prosecutor was the same as the last time, Parker told him. "Was she so happy with serving time that she wants to do it again? I can certainly arrange that if she wants."

No one laughed at his bad joke, and he cleared his throat. As he went on about how the witnesses had picked her out, how there were bloody fingerprints on the body and in the room, Tholan looked around.

There were a great many protectors around the room—not just the ones with their humans, but many of them on the ceiling, the walls, as well as sitting on tables. They had all grown to love his wife as much as he did, and wanted to see justice served. Tholan did as well.

"It says here that the body could not be found." The attorney nodded. "What exactly does that mean? I mean, how does one misplace a body? One that I myself signed the workorder on to have exhumed."

"Someone stole it." Judge Brown said that there had been a police person on duty with it since it was brought to the coroner's office. "That's what I mean. When it got to the office, there wasn't a body in the casket. Someone must have taken it."

Parker's attorney asked to approach the bench. He was one of the protectors that had been on this earth for a very long time and knew the law better than he would bet the judge did. Nolan James was good at his job.

"Anytime you'd like to join us, Peterson, that would make my day." Levi Peterson joined the other man at the judge's desk. They talked for several minutes, and then Judge Brown had them have a seat. He called to one of the officers at the back of the room. Whispering to him, he asked that there be a ten-minute recess while he had something checked out.

No one moved when the officer left. Tholan wasn't sure if it was because they didn't want to lose their seat or space, or if it didn't seem worth the effort to leave only to have to return.

Ten minutes later, the officer showed up. After a brief moment as Brown went over whatever had been brought to him, he looked around the room. Shaking his head, he asked Peterson if he wanted to stick to the stolen story.

"It's not a story. It's the truth. When we had the body removed, as you ordered, it was opened, and nothing was in the casket. I believe that Ms. Brooks had it removed so that she could get a mistrial. Well, it won't work. I know what sort of person she is."

"Do you now? From the test that was done on the casket, as well as the one I just had performed, the casket was never used. Never a body put inside. Nothing to indicate that anyone ever even put their hands on the silk pillow. So if, as you claim, she stole the body, how the hell did she steal it? There was nothing there to steal." Peterson said that wasn't possible. "Are you calling me a liar? I just told you, there wasn't a body inside it."

"Then the wrong body was exhumed."

Again, the officer came to the desk, and again he left for ten minutes. When he returned, he announced that thirty-four hundred and twelve was where the unknown was buried, and that was the body that had been exhumed.

"What is the name of this person that she killed? That would go a long way in helping your case too." Peterson, obviously in over his head, shuffled around some paperwork, then handed the judge another sheet of paper. While Peterson made a show of looking for the name, the judge read over the sheet.

When he laid it down, the judge asked for the doctor of Parker Daniel Brooks to be brought in. Peterson claimed that he was dead. The younger man that walked in looked very alive to Tholan and the rest of the courtroom.

"Sit down and shut up. You have done enough in the last half hour to make me think this entire thing was a railroad. But I'll go through the motions. I want to see how deeply you dig the hole that you're in before you tell me this was just what I said it was, a fuck up from day one." Doctor Cummings took the stand and stated that he was the partner of Doctor Cummings, his father, and physician to Mr. Brooks. "Tell me, young man. Is there any way that Mr. Brooks could have done this crime that he was accused of?"

"No, sir. He had been confined to a wheelchair since he'd been in an accident just before Parker was born. Her mother was killed, and the child taken from her at the hospital. Mr. Brooks survived, but with a severed spinal cord injury. I believe at the time of the supposed murder and robbery, he'd been in the chair for over twenty years." Peterson popped up out of his chair and said that Parker had been tried for the murder. "I have some information on that as well, Your Honor. Parker Brooks Daniels couldn't have committed the crime either. She was with me, on a date, when this accident was supposed to have occurred. I told the police that, several times, but they never brought me in as a witness. Neither did the attorney for Mrs. Daniels."

"So, she had an alibi, he was confined to a wheelchair, yet both of them were accused of this murder of a body that no one can find, and no one knows his name. And from the information that I just received, the building that this happened in hasn't been used for anything but a rat's home for the past forty years. How the hell you made this stick before is what I'd like to know."

"She confessed." Judge Brown asked Parker to stand up. When she did, Peterson said that this wasn't right, things were not being done correctly.

"If things had been done correctly the first time, I'm thinking, you'd have been fired by now, I'd be retired, and she'd be up here on this bench residing over stupid cases like this one. Of all the.... Did your momma drop you on your head when you were a baby? Or did you cheat at law school enough that you don't have the first clue what is right or wrong?" Brown looked at Parker and smiled. "Now, honey, you tell me, in your own words, why it is that you confessed to this charade that was going on."

"My da, as you heard, was confined to a wheelchair for most of his adult life. I knew, from being an attorney, that he'd never survive in prison. Not as an attorney, nor as a man that had been injured the way he was." She looked down, then up when she had picked up the contract between her stepmother and a man by the name of George Wilson. "My stepmother had signed a prenuptial agreement when they married. Shortly before this happened, my da had cut her off on spending. He had also filed for divorce from her. She orchestrated this whole thing to get him in prison, where he would be killed. If he was found guilty of a crime such as murder, Angela could have petitioned for the will that was made by my da to be null and void. She would have gotten everything."

He read over the paperwork that the bailiff brought to him. Judge Brown was shaking his head even before he finished. Looking at the other moron, what he'd been calling him since the second break, Judge Brown asked Peterson if he'd been a part of this.

"I was the one that found her guilty, yes. She got what she deserved." He asked him what that was. "Prison. It's no one's fault but her own that she confessed. Mr. Brooks would have been just fine behind bars."

This time when the judge asked for a recess, he left them all there. He said that it would be two hours, so they decided to get out and stretch their legs. When Parker came out, there were so many news crews there that they ended up inside the building again. She was pacing again when the bailiff came out to find them.

"Judge Brown, he'd like to talk to you both."

They followed the younger man, and when he stopped before opening the door, he told Parker that he was very sorry for her loss. It took him several seconds to realize he was talking about her stepmother, and not her father.

They entered the room just as Judge Brown picked up the ringing phone. He waved them to the seats and they both sat. Whatever was going on, Brown didn't seem all that happy about it. Tholan only hoped that the man would get what was coming to him; Peterson wasn't a good attorney at all.

~*~

"All to order."

Parker stood up with the rest of them. She still didn't know what was going on. After giving them her cell number, her identification at the jail, and verifying a copy of the will, she was asked to come back in a little while for the trial. Taking Tholan's hand into hers, she held it tightly while Judge Brown sat down.

"It has come to my attention, as it should have ten years ago, that there has been a miscarriage of justice. Mrs. Daniels gave up ten years of her life, her young life, for her father. Mr. Brooks died without his daughter by his side. All things that if you asked me, should never have happened. But they did, and there is nothing we can do about that now, I'm sorry to say. But I can do something now."

"Judge Brown, justice was served. She confessed to the crime and the state, as is its duty, prosecuted her to the fullest extent of the law." Judge Brown asked where the body was; where the blood was; the gun. "I don't know where they are. But that wasn't my job at the time. Nor is it now. It was to do

168

just what I did, put her in jail."

"Yes, so you did. And you really sucked at it then and now." Lifting up the paperwork that Judith had uncovered, Brown smiled at Peterson. "I have an amount in the form of a check from the bank account from one Joseph March, paid to the order of Levi Peterson of Maple Avenue for eighty-thousand dollars. In the note area, it even generously says 'payoff for D. Brooks.' How nice is that?" Levi sat down. Parker didn't think that he was expecting that. "I also have a check made out to the local police station, four different men, in an amount of forty thousand dollars each. They are currently being arrested. There is also a check written out to my former colleague, Robert Dunn. He was paid a sum of one hundred thousand dollars. That's going to put a crimp in his retirement, I'm thinking."

As he named off several more names and the amounts they'd been paid, Parker squeezed Tholan's hand. She was going to get justice, something that she'd been dreaming of for her da since she'd been arrested. When her name was said, Parker stood up, afraid that he'd found something more than they had.

"Mrs. Daniels, let me be the first to tell you how sorry I am that this happened to your family. I knew your father, and I always considered him a good friend and a better man. There was none like him, and I'm happy to have been a part of clearing his name and that of his daughter." Judge Brown stood up and moved toward her. "It is my greatest honor of all my life to give you this. You have been fully reinstated as an attorney. Your back pay is going to be given to you, as well as your record cleared of everything that you were stripped of. If I could bring back your father for you, I would do that as well. Congratulations."

Peterson was dragged away, kicking and screaming that he was being treated unfairly. Parker could feel her belly rumbling again, and she sat down. Tears, tears of happiness, filled her eyes as she looked down at one of the hardest things she'd ever worked for. Her diploma. Da had been so proud of her when she'd gotten it.

"Parker, if you don't have to run off right now, Hell and I have something for you too." She looked around. The only two people in the room with her and Boss were Tholan and Hell. She had a moment to worry that she was going to lose it all when Boss hugged her. "Such a worry wart. Hell will give you his first. Well, he's already given it to you, with my blessing, but I'll let him tell you."

"A woman such as yourself needs a child." She told him that she had one. "You do, and she will grow up to be a fine person like her mother. But I have, with Boss's permission, given you a child of your own. Not for what happened today, but for the fear of you that you have put into my demons. I don't think I've ever had a harder working group since I opened for business. Your son, yours and Tholan's, will be a good man, only surpassed by his father."

"A son?" Putting her hand over her belly, she looked at Tholan before asking Hell again. "You've given us a son? I don't understand."

"I owe you something, as I said, for what you did for me the other day. No one will bother your family, any of them, for as long as you are alive. Being an immortal, such as you all are, will mean that any child that you have or bring into your heart, and protector, mystic, or mates of such people, will be protected as well. And I swear to you, if there is ever a mishap, they will be dealt with quickly and only once."

Tholan hugged her when Hell left them. This would

170

explain why she was so ill. A baby. They were going to have a baby. Heather would be thrilled to death about it too.

"Now my gift for you. When you decided to help my people, you did so with great risk to yourself. You did this with the full knowledge that you could be harmed. And in doing so, you have given me as much as you have the men and women who work for me." She hugged Boss. "I'm not finished. What I have for you is only for an hour, I'm sorry to say. If I could make it longer, bring you this forever, I would. But too much time has passed. When you get home, your gift will be in the living room, and as soon as you see it, the countdown will begin. I don't have to tell you to use your time wisely."

Parker didn't want to go home. Whatever was there, it couldn't be as good as what she had right here. When Heather was picked up from school, she came with them to celebrate with a night out on the town to tell her about having a baby brother.

By midnight they were headed home. Having a lovely evening of dinner with friends and family, Parker was feeling much better. Even the sickness, now that she knew what was causing it, didn't bother her very much. Heather was as happy as they were to know that she'd be a big sister soon.

Tholan was telling Heather a knock-knock joke as they entered the house. Of course, he messed it up, and had them all laughing when they were hanging up jackets. Heather wasn't going to have class tomorrow, as it was a Saturday, and they were all going to sleep in.

Parker entered the living room to find someone there. She had started to yell for Maggie when he turned and looked at her.

"Da? Is that you?" He nodded and opened his arms.

171

Running to him, she nearly bowled him over when she hugged him. He was here. Her da was here. "I don't understand."

"I've come to see you, that's all. I can't stay, as you know." She started sobbing when he did. "My goodness, little girl, you've grown into a beautiful woman. I wouldn't have recognized you but for the freckles."

They hugged several more times before she remembered Tholan and Heather. She introduced her da to them, and he made over them both. When Heather and Tholan left them to visit, she sat down on the floor while he sat in his favorite chair.

"You're not in a wheelchair." He told her that he loved walking and did so daily. "Oh Da, I've missed you so much. My heart just wasn't into living anymore when I was told that you were gone. And now you're here, and I just don't know where to start in telling you things. Oh, I'm going to have a son. A baby, can you believe it?"

"I was told. Boss, a very nice man, he told me that I could be there when he was brought into the world. That for a few seconds before he takes his first breath, I can touch him." Parker cried for all that he was going to miss, how much he had already. "Don't cry, my darling. I'm happy and free of pain. And now that my little girl is going to be a momma of her own, and an attorney, you cannot believe how thrilled I am to be given this opportunity to just touch you again."

They talked the entire hour. And when the bell on the front clock chimed twice, she knew that it was time for him to go. Holding his hand tighter, she told him over and over how much she loved him.

"I have something that I want to tell you before I leave you. Something that I should have said to you more often. I'm so very proud of you, PJ. I have been since you were laid in my arms in that hospital bed that dreary day. Every day you brought joy to my heart, love to my soul, and you made me think. Not just about the future, but the past as well." Parker couldn't speak around the lump in her throat. "I know that over the years I told you that we would work together on making ourselves comfortable, so that we'd never have to do without. But it was for you, PJ. Every decision that I made, every dollar that came in, it was all for you. I never wanted you to have to worry about anything at any time. And when you were taken from me, I made sure that you could and would come back to it. And that it would be safe for you."

"I love you, Da. I wish we had more time." He told her that they had forever, that he was with her all the time. "But I can't see you. I want to look at you and tell you how things are going."

"Oh honey, you will be able to. When that little man of yours comes into this world, it will be me that you're looking upon. I will be there with him — I will be the one that whispers in his ears. Not his protector, but someone more important. I'm going to be his grandda. His one and only."

Long after he left her, Parker sat on the living room floor. She could smell him still. His cologne was still lingering in the room. His voice echoed in her mind and heart. Parker promised herself that never would a day go by that she didn't tell her children about the greatest grandda in the world. They'd know Parker Daniel Brooks as well as she did, because she was going to make sure of it.

When the chimes of the clock struck again, Parker made her way up to their bedroom. Tholan was on their bed, reading a book, and Heather was curled up beside him. It looked as if he had been reading to her about the Robinson family and their trials, and she'd fallen asleep, but Tholan kept reading.

For all she knew, he might have known the author.

Crawling in to be with her little family, she held her daughter while Tholan read to her too. Before long, she was sound asleep. And there were no demons to bother her ever again.

Chapter 12

Fifteen years later, Christmas season

Tholan watched his love as she danced on the stage. He knew better than to try and keep up with her with his camera. She was beautifully fast, skimming over the stage. But she was stunning, and she knew the steps to the music like she did her own name. When the dance she was in came to an end, he knew that he'd have just enough time to go to the back room and hug her before the rest of the actors and dancers beat him to it. His daughter, Heather, had danced into the hearts of so many, but she only held his heart in her own. For now, anyway.

Hugging her tightly, Tholan told her, as he did every time he came to see her perform, that she'd been the best on stage. And just like all the times before, she told him that he was silly. When her mom and the rest of her siblings joined them, Tholan stood back and allowed them time with the star of the show.

"I'm sort of sad that this is the last night of the show." It was Christmas Eve, and the entire family had taken an entire floor of a hotel in New York to watch Heather's last night on stage this year. "But the good news is, I've been asked to come back and try out next year."

She'd be the star again, and Tholan wanted to tell her that, but to do so, he knew, would jinx it for her. He had no idea why she thought that, but he had learned to keep his opinions to himself when it came to her and dancing.

As they were leaving the theater, Brooks, her little brother, told her that he had gotten her some flowers. But like Tholan, he'd left them at the hotel. As they were trying to cross the street, the traffic heavy even for as late as it was, Tholan kept an eye on his family.

He had four daughters now and two boys, one of those his biological son. But they were all, as far as he and Parker were concerned, a biological part of them. Each of them had come to the two of them with some sort of issue, from being abused to just being abandoned. Brooks was the only infant that they'd ever had — again, so far.

Dinner was a late affair tonight. As they took their seats, he noticed that not only was Michael there, but also Boss. Hugging them all, Heather flew from one person to the next before Parker was able to get her to have a seat. After Boss left them, claiming that he had work to do, Michael sat for a time and told them how much he'd enjoyed the play. He'd never seen it before.

"I have decided that I shall try and get time to see more of such things. It's calming, is it not, just to watch the story unfold? I have known the author of the play you were in, Heather, and I think that even he would have enjoyed the way that you and the troupe brought it to life."

A greater compliment couldn't have been given. When he

too left them, they settled into their meals and laughed and talked loudly.

Tholan couldn't believe how much his life had changed over the years. He had a wonderful family, a wife that he loved more than he could ever have thought possible, and children. And just yesterday, he and Parker had been asked to take on three more children for the holidays, and more than likely forever. It was what they did. Take them in, settle them, and if they could, move them to family. That was the hardest on Parker.

As they were leaving the restaurant, the traffic hadn't changed at all. The snow coming down made for slick driving and walking, and he was extra careful with his wife. Parker was the love of his life, but so clumsy in the snow. As they were trying to get their footing after one little slide, Tholan looked up when he heard screams and tires squealing.

Heather was standing in front of a long limo—not theirs, but one similar. She was screaming at the driver, telling him to watch the lights and that they were walking there, when out of nowhere, a person came and bumped her in the back. With the slippery snow and ice, she went down like she'd been dropped from a mountain, hitting her head on the asphalt.

He didn't move. His heart stopped beating for several seconds. Blood was spreading on the road beneath her. And before he could move, her protector touched her hand to her and Tholan rushed to them.

"No. Don't touch her." He must have looked mad; no one but his family and himself could see the woman. "Don't take her. She's my little girl."

Parker felt for her pulse and screamed. She was gone? His prima donna was gone? Trying to get closer to her—the people were blocking his way—Tholan too fell to the road as he watched his little girl's soul speak to her protector. No. No, this could not be happening. Not to his children. They were immortal. Trying again to get to her, he felt a heavy hand on his shoulder and turned to look at Boss.

"Leave her be." Tholan shook his head. "You must leave her be, Tholan. I have this under control."

"This is my punishment. You have taken my child for what I did so long ago." He said nothing, but Tholan wanted answers. "You can take me. I will go with you. Just leave my child here. I beg of you."

"Tholan?" He turned to look at Parker, who was still sitting in the blood and snow. "Tholan, he's saving her."

There was a man standing over Heather, packing snow in her wounds, talking to her while he worked. His words were not important, but what he was doing seemed to be helping. And when she inhaled sharply, her body rising up from the concrete, Tholan dropped to his knees and cried. She was his, she was back.

"I believe that she will not be yours any longer, Tholan." He looked at Boss, who nodded to his daughter. "This is the man that I have set to marry her. She will bring you grandchildren, and they more children. It was what I had hoped for you all along."

"How did she...? She wasn't breathing." Boss winked at him. "You planned this—for me?"

"Nay, never. I would never be so cruel as that. But, as you have seen over the decades, for every mistake, there has to be something to balance it. This was the balance from so long ago. Not that it was meant for you, but for her. She will need this more than you will ever be...well, you might be able to believe it. You have your own Parker, don't you?"

The ambulance came twenty minutes later—the traffic

had slowed it. And if not for the young man with Heather, Tholan wasn't sure what else might have befallen her. As she was loaded into the large van, Parker got in and he started to as well. But he turned to the young man—his name was David—and told him that he should go.

"No, that's fine, I'll follow in my car." They both looked at the traffic, backed up more now with the accident. "Yes, well, I might be a while. She might be out of school by then."

"She's been out of school for some time. Heather, she's a dancer." David looked at Heather, then at him. "Go. You saved her for us. It's only fitting that you go. And the hospital might have questions of you. Go. I will be there as soon as I can."

David got into the ambulance and it roared away. Tholan's heart felt like a little piece of it was broken away when he realized what he'd done. He'd just okayed for his baby to fall in love. Tholan let out a long breath.

Gathering the rest of his family up, they were loaded into their limo only five minutes later and on their way. A shortcut had somehow been found, and they were only thirty minutes behind the ambulance, but Heather was already in surgery by then. David Sanders, medical doctor and surgeon, was the one in there with her. Tholan sat with Parker in the waiting room as they awaited word on what was going to be happening.

"She's his mate, isn't she?" He nodded, his heart just not ready for this right now. "Oh, Tholan. We knew this would happen someday. I'm just sorry to see it happen so soon."

"Yes, well, Brooks pointed out to me that she is a little long in the tooth to be not married. I think that he's been hanging out with Valyn too much. That man must have a book of quotes that he's picked up over the decades." They both laughed and watched the others sit quietly. "We've been very lucky, I think. I'm not saying that we've had it on easy street, but I think we've done more than most have."

"Having love in our hearts and a seemingly endless supply of money has helped too. Maggie and I figured it up the other day—we've had forty-seven children in our lives in the last fifteen years, and only a few of them—one or two, we think—that we couldn't save." Parker laid her head on his shoulder as she continued. "Tholan, what will we do without her in our home? I don't want to have her move away."

His heart hurt for lost children. They had been raised by terrible beings, and no amount of love or understanding had helped. One had died due to drugs; the other was in prison for bank robbery. But with their daughter, they could fix that.

"We'll buy them a home. Close to where we live." She looked at him and frowned. "I've been getting really good at being stern. Perhaps I can use a bit of it on him to make him move close to us."

"Yes, because that has worked so well on Heather. I'm sure that compared to her, he'll be a pushover." They laughed again and stood up when a nurse joined them in the room. "Is she all right?"

"Yes, Dr. Sanders just wanted to make sure that there wasn't anything inside the wound before he stitched it up. And he also wanted me to tell you that she should be in recovery in about twenty minutes. If you'd like to get some coffee or something, I can call you when she's ready." They said that they'd wait, they didn't drink coffee. "He's a good doctor. His last day was today, and him being right there where she needed him, it was a miracle. Some doctors would have just stitched.... Never mind. Anyway, we're going to miss him. He's moving to Ohio, soon to retire. He said that he needs a rest."

When the nurse left, he and Parker looked at each other and burst out laughing. Of course, it was a miracle, and that he was moving to Ohio. Heather wouldn't be moving that far away after all. Of course, he took credit for the doctor taking an early retirement.

As soon as they could, they sent the others back to the hotel. New York might be the city that never sleeps, but the children did need it. Going into Heather's room, being led there by the nurse, Parker and Tholan walked in on Dr. Sanders sitting on the bed, talking to Heather, and they were holding hands.

"Dad, Mom, you remember David, don't you? He was in one of my classes at college. English Lit. I had him come home with me that first Thanksgiving that his parents were away." They shook hands, and Tholan felt the connection to him all the way to his heart. "His parents are getting a divorce, and he's decided that he can't take the bickering anymore. He's sold his house and is moving to our town. Isn't that wonderful?"

"Yes, it is."

Tholan noticed that David didn't release Heather's hand, and he wasn't really sure how he felt about that. Of course, they were going to be mates, but she had been theirs first. When Parker took his hand in hers, he knew she was trying to make him behave. He'd only just realized that he'd been glaring at their hands.

"Heather has a nasty bump on her head, and I'm going to keep her here for a few hours more. She should be home in time for Christmas dinner. And I hope you don't mind, but she asked me to come along too." Parker told him that he was more than welcome. "Thank you very much. That's the one thing that I remember most about the two of you — you were

181

always the politest people, and you would open your doors to anyone. Thank you for that."

"It's what makes us happy. To have family and friends around all the time." Parker grinned at him. "Heather said that you were moving to Ohio? Have you a house yet? We have two near us. I'm not being pushy or anything, but they're nice homes."

"Really?" David looked at Heather and she nodded. "Heather and I are going to start seeing each other. I mean, seeing a bit more of each other. We did date a bit in college, but...to be honest with you, I'm already about halfway in love with her. And she just told me that she's thought of me often too."

"Good, then it's settled. The houses are near us but not too close, and we've just had them both cleaned up and painted, trying to get them off the market. This could not be better." Parker stood up, and Tholan did as well as she continued. "All right, love. We will come for you, unless David will be bringing you to the hotel. Good then, we'll see you today. Your father and I, we have lots to do, and I need a nap."

After kissing her on the cheek, they both left. Tholan looked at Parker when they were in the elevator and cocked a brow at her. They didn't have any houses, they hadn't had anything cleaned up, and as far as he knew, the market for such houses was very good.

"Oh, all right, I said a few fibs. But a few phone calls and it will be as right as rain." Tholan said nothing. "Bear with me on this, Tholan, I can't stand the thought of our daughter too far away any more than you can. So, I fibbed. I'll make it right. You'll see."

"Of that, I have no doubt." Parker was making calls as soon as they were in the limo again. "I love you, Parker

Daniels."

By the time they were in their rooms, not only did she have three houses that were being worked on, but one of them was next to them. The crew would start on them first thing the day after New Year's—that was how long they were staying in New York—and it would be ready by the time they arrived. Tholan wasn't sure who was happier, him or the kids. They loved Heather too.

~*~

Heather was in love. And as she sat as quietly as she could on the couch at the hotel, she couldn't stop staring at the man next to her on the floor. He was everything that she could have hoped for in a man, and he'd told her on the way here that he had fallen in love with her as well.

It was fast, she would admit that. But then all the mates to the protectors had— She thought of something and sat there stunned for several seconds before she heard the laughter in her head. Boss.

Yes, I planned this. Are you well? She said that she was, and that she was happy. *As it should be. David is a good man, as you know. A few things that he's working on—his parents have never been kind. It's difficult for him to take in in that your family is so loving.*

I love him. He said that it was in her mind just how much she did. *My dad told me the story once, of Elizabeth. Is this his payback for that?*

No. He asked the same thing when you lay on the road. I would never do that. Never. But there has to be a balance. As you are aware. She told him that she was. *You will have many children and be as happy as your parents are now. This is what I wanted for you, we all did. You are special to us, Heather, to all protectors. You brought Tholan to us all, you and Parker.*

183

I don't understand. He explained it to her. *But I thought that would have been Brooks, their real son. I mean, I know I was the first, but that doesn't make sense.*

You are all their biological children as far as they're concerned. None of you have ever thought of them as adoptive parents. Not one child that has come through them, even the ones that failed them, haven't learned something from them, taken it to their hearts. She knew that as well. *Yes, when you visit Billy in prison, is he not a redeemed man? Did he not tell you that he was going to come out of prison and change his life? That is because of you, through the love of your parents. Did you know that they visit him as well?*

Yes, he told me. She looked around the room, at the gifts that had been opened, the paper that was stacked near the trash cans. The tree that had been put in the room by the hotel staff. *Boss, will David ever die?*

No, I could no more do that to you than I could have taken you from Parker and Tholan. All of you are immortals. And now that you have reached your age, neither you nor David will age. You will be together for all time. She squeezed David's hand when he kissed the back of it. *You enjoy your day with family, my child. I wish you all the luck in the world, you know that.*

The day was spent with David, and when his parents called, each of them leaving him messages, he ignored them, which she was happy about. They would be a part of their lives, she knew this. But Heather, like her mom, would lay down some rules, and they'd either follow them or she'd have to show them what sort of wife she was going to be to David. And she would be his wife, just as soon as she could. Life, even for an immortal, was too short to let things get in the way.

Napping lightly in her room, she wasn't surprised when David joined on her the bed. He held her tightly, telling her what a good time he'd had today, and she drifted off knowing that forever, this would be a favorite day.

When she woke she was alone in the big bed, but she knew that David hadn't left. He told her that he was going to travel to Ohio with them. Getting up slowly, she made her way to the bathroom and looked in the mirror.

The freckles that she'd had since childhood were still there. Her red hair, pulled back in a ponytail, was still as flaming as it had ever been. Getting into the shower, she scrubbed herself twice, careful of the stitches in her head. When she was finished, like her parents could, Heather dressed herself in comfy clothing and walked into the bedroom. David was there waiting for her. She knew that something had happened.

"Will you marry me?" Nodding at him, he smiled, but looked no less worried. "My parents are coming here today. Both of them. I had hoped that we could gently ease them into the family, but that's not going to happen, I guess. I told them I was marrying you if you said yes, and they are coming en masse to meet you and your family. I don't want them here, as you can well imagine, but there was no stopping them."

"We can deal with them as a family. I don't know if you noticed this or not, but we're not pushovers." He laughed. It cleared up his worry lines, and she was happy for that. "Have you told my parents and family yet? And warned them to not murder them?"

"As much as I'd like to say that I should have warned them, I didn't. I don't really think that your parents have a mean bone in their bodies. But they do know that my parents are coming. You know what Brooks said? He'd protect me. That kid.... I really love your family, Heather. All of them." She said that they loved him as well. "This is so fast, don't you think? I mean, I wouldn't change it for the world, but this is so fast."

"No. And before your parents get here, there are a few things that you should know." He said that her dad had told him. "Everything? Or just the stuff he thought you could handle right now. Dad would be like that, gently letting you know."

"Funny thing is — oh, he told me everything, I think — I knew back then that you were different than any other family. The wings, I have to admit, those sort of freaked me out a bit. But everything else, that was just like telling me that there was snow coming. I sort of had it in the back of my mind that whatever you were, I'd get that too." She said that he had. "Good. I love you. And I have a ring for you. Your mom gave it to me."

She looked at the ring, so much like her parents' that she cried. Boss had done this for them too. And when David slipped it on her finger, it fit as well as her clothing did. Her hand filled with something, and Heather opened her palm to find his ring.

"I'm not even going to ask. But I do have a feeling that we'll not just be engaged but married too." Heather asked David if that would bother him if it were true. "No, not the least bit. I love you, Heather Sanders. And will for the rest of our days together."

Kissing, they held each other for a long time. Then they laid back on her bed and talked. They didn't really make any hard decisions, but they did both want children, they wanted the house next to her parents, and they were also going to adopt. Nothing concrete, but just making a plan. Just as they needed.

At eight o'clock his parents showed up. Heather was ready for them, and so was her family. When they came in the door, bickering and telling David that he was stupid—yes, stupid—she walked right up to them and told them to shut the fuck up. That got their attention right away.

"Now. We will be calm and speak in our inside voices. If not, then you can leave. This is my family and our hotel room. If you want to be assholes and scream, then you can do that at your own home. Not here." Mr. Sanders stood up and said that she'd not talk to him that way. "Yes, I will. You'll find that I am not a person that you want to mess with, under any circumstances, and if you try, you'll see the back of our door more often than the other side. I do not suffer fools, and if you want to be one, then I guess that is going to suck for you."

"David, are you going to let this...this woman talk to us this way? We're your parents, for Christ's sake." David stood up and took her hand. Heather waited. This was going to be the point where his parents would either run all over them or not. "I will not allow this. Not so long as I have breath in my body will I allow someone to talk to me that way."

"Then, as Heather said, it will suck for you. And so you know, we were married today. I just couldn't wait to have her in my life as my wife." His mother sputtered about time and divorce. "Never. I won't ever divorce her. She is the love of my life, the woman that I've been waiting for. And if you cause us any trouble, any grief, then you will be barred from our home, and our children. I won't have you being negative around them or us. It's up to you."

"This is uncalled for. I demand that you come back to the estate with us and we'll discuss your options, and how you're going to take care of the two of us now that we've decided to divorce. I won't have you treating us like this, just because you've been getting some pussy." Heather moved toward Mr. Sanders. "What? You don't think I'm telling it—?"

Using a little — just a tiny bit — of her magic, she punched him in the face. And when he fell back, landing on his ass, she turned to Mrs. Sanders. Enough was enough.

"Get out of here. And take this sack of shit with you. If you ever again talk to me or my family like you just have, then I will take care that you never darken our doorstep again." Mrs. Sanders asked if she was threatening her. "No. I'm telling you a fact. Now get out and be glad that I'm allowing the two of you to leave here on your own. David, help your father, if you would. Your parents are just leaving."

David was laughing when he helped his father up, laughed as he escorted them to the elevator, and he was still laughing when he came back, pulled her into his arms, and told her how much he loved her. Heather was glad now that she'd listened to her heart and set the ground rules for her life.

Epilogue

Tholan looked around the room. There were so many people here that he was glad now that they'd decided to have the wedding outside instead of renting a large hall. He didn't think there was one big enough for this sort of thing anyway. He looked back at Brooks when he called to him.

"Dad, do you think she'll be there? I mean, she's not run off, has she?" He straightened his tie and told him that she would never do that. "I can't believe that I'm getting married. But I also can't believe she said yes."

"It was meant to be." Brooks, now twenty-four, had met his mate. And now, in a large ceremony that her parents had insisted on, he was going to be leaving the nest too. "You've talked to her, haven't you? About the house?"

"I did, and I have to tell you, Dad, her parents are really upset about it. They wanted us to live near them. I don't think that would have worked out so well, do you?" He held his tongue. It was difficult with Brooks's new family, but they'd work it out. "Heather told me what to say to them. I think, like she did, it made them respect me more. Doubtful that it'll last, but I don't care so long as Margo is in my life."

"Good for you. Have a seat and try not to fidget so much. I can't believe I still have to tell you that. We have about an hour before it starts, and I'm just going to step out for a moment. David is here if you need something." When Brooks nodded, Tholan stepped out of the tent and into the yard where everyone was still mingling.

David had fathered four grandchildren for him, and Heather was having a fifth. Tholan thought grandchildren were more fun than anything. And he loved them so very much.

Looking at the group there, he thought of all the men that had come before him as a mystic. All of them had children and grandchildren — some, great grandchildren. But they still worked on the compound, and still trained the new protectors every day.

Riss and Kala had retired. They had wanted to see the world and had left the compound in the hands of their oldest son. There had been improvements, not only to the equipment that they used but also the way that they were being trained. Cell phones had been a big issue, and they'd had to work around them for a long time now. Tholan had one, but sometimes would forget where he'd put it. He thought perhaps it was because he didn't like it. It was too connected to things.

Judith still ran her shop, though like Riss and Kala, she too had taken some time off. Not that she didn't still make things — Tholan didn't think she'd ever be able to stop doing that — but she and Agon would travel the world looking for herbs, new and old, and to try new foods. That was what they had wanted to do for a while now, and Tholan was glad that they'd gotten some time to do it. But he had a feeling that they'd be back at the ovens soon enough.

Galin had stayed at the compound. Tholan thought it was because he enjoyed the new recruits that he could tell jokes to—he was good at them, too. His delivery was spot on, and he never messed up. Tholan still couldn't tell a joke well, and even the stupid book of knock-knock ones had been a failure. Galin had given up trying to help him with them.

Kip had gone on to college and gotten a law degree. He worked with Parker on cases, the two of them making quite the name for themselves. Dusty still helped with the computer things. He'd never seen another person who could find things that no one else did on them. She was thrilled to be helping Kip, and Parker as well.

Renie ran the local grade school. She had been nicknamed The Enforcer, and she loved it. But children were safe in her school. They were also fed well, had book bags and supplies every year, and no one was left out when projects were bought in. They loved her despite her nickname. Tholan even took to calling her that at meetings he'd have with her.

Arryn, too, had stayed with the compound. He worked with the animal watchers and told them ways to use their time wisely. He also made sure that they had rest when they were finished for the night, even if they only had to sit on a swing and sway back and forth. Tholan had thought it silly until he sat on one for an hour and felt like the weight of the world had been lifted from his shoulders.

Valyn, still a jokester, had left the compound altogether some years ago. He worked in town trying to get new businesses to come in. The employment rate was at an all-time low of less than one percent, and Jenny, his wife, was trying to get him to run for a high office position. Her way of thinking was that if he could do that for their town, he could

191

do so much more for the entire state.

Jenny worked at the nursing homes and hospitals still, bringing books and treats for all those that wanted them. And she still sat with families when they lost someone, as well as would spell them a while when they'd been waiting. That, Tholan thought, was the hardest on her — sitting with a family that was waiting for their loved one to pass on.

Tholan didn't work at all, not outside the home anyway. He would occasionally help out at the compound when needed, but he was a stay at home daddy. They didn't have small children at the house right now, but he would go to get them when needed. A shed had been put up, and it was stocked with things that all newborns might need, and older children too, from diapers and clothing to strollers and baby beds. Car seats were bought when needed, to keep them up to date on all the laws.

Parker worked with Boss. And sometimes, when he needed just a few hours to himself, she would sit at his big desk and take care of things. It relaxed the man, and gave him a much-needed reprieve, as well as time to catch up on things like riding rollercoasters and shopping. Boss had become quite the shopper, even online at times. When he thought of the gifts that they'd gotten last year, he had to laugh. Boss should really read the description before handing gifts out from now on. It was funny but embarrassing as well.

Tholan looked at Heather, heavy with child, and her husband, David. He had become a renowned surgeon over the years, called by other hospitals to come in and show them how to do a particular procedure. He told him once that with age comes practice. Tholan thought that by the time the man was his age, he'd be perfect at anything.

David's parents had died not long after Heather had their

first child. They had never made up with them, were never allowed to visit their home. The one and only time that they had been invited, they had drawn guns on each other and had to be arrested. That was the straw that broke the back, Tholan thought. His parents died alone in their respective homes, never having laid eyes on any of their grandchildren. "Natural causes" was what the reports said, but Tholan thought it was loneliness. He knew firsthand what that could be like.

When he was told there were only five minutes to go, he went back into the little tent and told them all to be ready. The men lined up, and Tholan made his way to Parker so that they could be seated with the rest of the people there. And when the music sounded that the bride was coming out, everyone stood up and watched her make her way to the front of the large gathering.

Before she made it there, however, she stopped where they were seated. Letting go of her father, who was giving her away, she pulled Parker to her first, kissing her on the cheek, then did the same to him. But she pulled them both out of their seats and brought them to the front with the rest of the wedding party. Then she cleared her throat before speaking.

"Today I marry the greatest man I have ever known, with the exception of my own father. And with that, I am marrying into the sweetest family that a woman could have ever been a part of. When Brooks asked me to marry him, the entire clan of Daniels cheered with me. They cried when my mom passed away when Brooks and I were newly engaged, even though they'd not known her well." She looked at the two of them as she continued to address the guests. "Several days ago, I will admit I got cold feet. I was sure that Brooks was making the biggest mistake of his life in marrying me. I mean, really, who am I but just a waitress that he met at a family gathering? Oh, and they tip well too. Very well."

Everyone laughed, but she wasn't finished. "Parker sat me down and slapped me gently on the cheek. I was shocked, but also knew to pay attention to her. She told me that there was one person in this world for each of us, and we only got one chance to make it right for us. Parker told me that I was luckier than most in that I found my true love when I did. Brooks was set to move away the next day and canceled his plans to be with me." Margo hugged Parker. "I could have canceled, she told me, and she'd take care of it all. But she also told me to close my eyes and try to imagine my life without Brooks. Getting up in the morning and not having his blueberry waffles. To think about what it would be like to watch Ohio State alone. To go to bed without his side being filled and his pillow smelling like him. I couldn't do it. So, here I am today."

Margo looked at him then, and he was almost afraid of what she'd say. "Tholan told me once that Brooks had been a gift to them. He told me that he and Parker knew that they'd have no children of their own, but one day, Parker found out that she was with child. And that they decided right then that their life couldn't be more complete. Then he told me how I had come into their lives, like the other spouses of their children, and filled spaces in their hearts when they thought it was full. He told me every day after that that he was and forever will be the luckiest man alive to have been blessed with so many people that loved him."

After she hugged him, he started to sit down with Parker. But Brooks pulled him up beside him and said that he wanted them there. That they were going to be just as much Margo's family as they were his. And while the two of them were pronounced man and wife, he and Parker kissed as well. It

194

could not have been a happier ending of a wedding.

There were so many gifts to the couple that they'd been stored in the house. Two rooms of them, all of them in the prettiest shades of gold and silver that he'd ever seen. As he walked through the rooms, admiring the love that people had bestowed upon his children, he noticed one package, sitting in the middle of all the beautiful wrappings, that was in the deepest shade of red that he'd ever seen. He didn't have to look to see who it was from.

"Dad? Margo and I were just— What's that?" He handed the package to his son, as his name was the only one on it. "Is this a joke? I mean, who gives a gift to the married man?"

"Open it." Brooks tore the paper off and stared into the box for so long, he was nervous. Brooks looked at him before reaching inside and pulling out a scroll like parchment that was also wrapped in a red ribbon. "Is this from Hell?"

"I think so." Brooks, like all the children, knew about Hell. They hadn't ever seen him, nor had they talked to him, but they knew that he'd been the one that had given them the gift of Brooks. When he peeled off the ribbon, he opened the scroll up and laughed.

It was a drawing, of Hell himself. Brooks had drawn it when he'd been no more than three years old, right after they'd told him the story about his coming to them. When a small scrap of paper hit the floor, Tholan bent to pick it up. Handing it to Brooks, he read it to him.

"I have taken the liberty of giving you a bit of money. I have no need for it, and I wanted you to have it. Do not, under any circumstances, think that I'm doing a good deed. It's just money that I have no use for. Have a good life, Brooks, and have lots of children." It was signed with a single H.

After the kids had left on their honeymoon, Tholan told

Parker what had happened. She laughed about the good deed too as they made their way up to their bedroom. In the morning they'd have a crew come in and clean up for them. But for now, they needed to rest.

Tholan laid by his Parker and picked up his latest romance book. Kathi Barton was becoming one of his all-time favorites.

Before You Go...

HELP AN AUTHOR

write a review

THANK YOU!

Share your voice and help guide other readers to these wonderful books. Even if it's only a line or two your reviews help readers discover the author's books so they can continue creating stories that you'll love. Login to your favorite retailer and leave a review. Thank you.

AWARD WINNING, BESTSELLING AUTHOR

Kathi Barton, winner of the Pinnacle Book Achievement award as well as a best-selling author on Amazon and All Romance books, lives in Nashport, Ohio with her husband Paul. When not creating new worlds and romance, Kathi and her husband enjoy camping and going to auctions. She can also be seen at county fairs with her husband who is an artist and potter.

Her muse, a cross between Jimmy Stewart and Hugh Jackman, brings her stories to life for her readers in a way that has them coming back time and again for more. Her favorite genre is paranormal romance with a great deal of spice. You can visit Kathi online and drop her an email if you'd like. She loves hearing from her fans. aaronskiss@gmail.com.

Follow Kathi on her blog: http://kathisbartonauthor.blogspot.com/

www.ingramcontent.com/pod-product-compliance
Lightning Source LLC
Chambersburg PA
CBHW030222180626
46810CB00008B/2921